W9-CLH-209

PRAISE FOR
ON THE NATURE OF HUMAN ROMANTIC INTERACTION

"Iagnemma's desperate, comic, and determined heroes seek, with beautiful futility, formulas for love, loss, history, religion, and odd arts. Here are crackpots and lovelorn, bewildered geniuses, sincerely seeking impossible truths. These are wonderful stories, and Karl Iagnemma is one of our very best young writers."
—Brad Watson, National Book Award finalist and author of *The Heaven of Mercury*

"Karl Iagnemma's stories are carefully written and beautifully detailed in their investigations of people caught up in the webs of science and history, and they dramatize, with great precision, the traps that the mind and body can sometimes stumble into. He is affectionate and severe about his chosen territory, the Midwest: this is a fine book." —Charles Baxter, author of *The Feast of Love*

"[A] mature voice, distinctive style and broad perspective helps Iagnemma shape the refreshing imaginative territory he explores." —*The Philadelphia Inquirer*

"A spellbinding collection . . . Iagnemma evokes raw emotion as his characters reconcile their reliance on scientific facts with their need for the intangible, transient qualities of love." —*Discover* magazine

ON THE NATURE OF

HUMAN ROMANTIC

INTERACTION

KARL IAGNEMMA

A DIAL PRESS TRADE PAPERBACK

ON THE NATURE OF HUMAN ROMANTIC INTERACTION
A Dial Press Trade Paperback

PUBLISHING HISTORY
Dial Press hardcover edition published May 2003
Delta trade paperback edition / July 2004
Dial Press trade paperback edition / July 2005

Published by Bantam Dell
A Division of Random House, Inc.
New York, New York

Cover image of apple © Hans Neleman/Getty Images
Cover image of robed figure © Rosanne Olson/Graphistock

Book design by Lynn Newmark

The following stories appeared in somewhat different form in the following publications:
"On the Nature of Human Romantic Interaction" and "The Confessional Approach" in
The Paris Review; "Zilkowski's Theorem" and "The Phrenologist's Dream" in *Zoetrope:
All Story;* "The Indian Agent" in *Meridian;* "The Ore Miner's Wife" in *The Virginia
Quarterly Review;* "Children of Hunger" in *One Story;* and "Kingdom, Order, Species" in
The Antioch Review. "On the Nature of Human Romantic Interaction" will be reprinted
in *The Pushcart Prize 2003: Best of the Small Presses.* "Zilkowski's Theorem" appeared in
Best American Short Stories 2002. "On the Nature of Human Romantic Interaction" was
the recipient of the 2001 *Paris Review* Discovery Prize.

The excerpts from the fictional book *Woody Plants* that appear on pages 129, 134, 136, and
145 are reprinted from *Michigan Trees: A Guide to the Trees of Michigan and the Great
Lakes Region,* by Burton Verve Barnes and Warren H. Wagner, Jr., copyright 1981, with
the permission of the University of Michigan Press.

Library of Congress Catalog Card Number: 2003040953

The Dial Press and Dial Press Trade Paperbacks are registered trademarks of
Random House, Inc., and the colophon is a trademark of Random House, Inc.

ISBN 0-385-33594-6

Manufactured in the United States of America
Published simultaneously in Canada

BVG   10   9   8   7   6   5   4   3   2

To my parents, and my sisters

CONTENTS

ON THE NATURE OF

HUMAN ROMANTIC

INTERACTION

WHEN students here can't stand another minute, they get drunk and hurl themselves off the top floor of the Gehring building, the shortest building on campus. The windows were tamper-proofed in August, so the last student forced open the roof access door and screamed *Fuck!* and dove spread-eagled into the night sky. From the TechInfo office I watched his body rip a silent trace through the immense snow dunes that ring the Gehring building. A moment later he poked his head from a dune, dazed and grinning, and his four nervous frat brothers whooped and dusted him off and carried him on their shoulders to O'Dooley's, where they bought him shots of Jaegermeister until he was so drunk he slid off his stool and cracked his teeth against the stained oak bar.

In May a freshwoman named Deborah Dailey heaved a chair through a plate-glass window on the fifth floor of the Gray building, then followed the chair down to the snowless parking lot, shattering both ankles and fracturing her skull. Later we learned—unsurprisingly—that her act had something to do with love: false love, failed love, mistimed or misunderstood or miscarried love. For no one here, I'm convinced, is truly happy in love. This is the Institute: a windswept quadrangle edged by charm-proofed concrete buildings. The sun disappears in October and temperatures drop low enough to flash-freeze saliva; spit crackles against the pavement like hail. In January whiteouts shut down the highways, and the outside world takes on a quality very much like oxygen: we know it exists all around us, but we can't see it. It's a disturbing thing to be part of. My ex–Ph.D. adviser, who's been here longer than any of us, claims that the dormitory walls are abuzz with frustration, and if you press your ear against the heating ducts at night you can hear the jangling bedsprings and desperate whimpers of masturbators. Some nights my ex-adviser wanders the subbasement hallways of the Gray building, and screams obscenities until he feels refreshed and relatively tranquil.

I used to be a Ph.D. student, but now my job is to sit all night at a government-issue desk in the TechInfo office, staring at a red TechHotline telephone. The TechHotline rings at three and four A.M., and I listen to distraught graduate students stammer about corrupted file allocation tables and SCSI controller failures. I tell them to close their eyes and take a deep breath; I tell them everything will be all right. The TechInfo office looks onto the quadrangle, and just before dawn, when the sky has mellowed to the color of a deep bruise, the Institute looks almost peaceful. At those rare moments I love my job and I love this town and I love this Institute. This is an indisputable fact:

there are many, many people around here who love things that will never love them back.

A Venn diagram of my love for Alexandra looks like this:

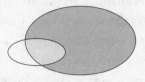

My inventory of love is almost completely consumed by Alexandra, while hers is shared by myself and others (or, more precisely: $|J| > |M|$; $\exists x\ s.t.\ x \in (J \cap M)$; $\exists y\ s.t.\ y \in J,\ y \notin M$; $\exists \zeta$ $s.t.\ \zeta \notin J,\ \zeta \in M$). We live in a cabin next to the Owahee River and the Institute's research-grade nuclear power plant. Steam curls off the hyperboloidal cooling tower and settles in an icy mist on our roof, and some nights I swear I can see the reactor building glowing. Alexandra has hair the color of maple syrup, and she is sixteen years younger than me; she is twenty-five. She sips tea every morning in the front room of our cabin, and when I turn into the driveway and see her hair through the window I feel a deep, troubling urge.

Alexandra is the daughter of my ex-adviser, who has never claimed to be happy in love. On Wednesdays at noon he meets a sophomore named Larissa in the Applied Optics Laboratory and scoots her onto the vibration isolation table and bangs her until the air pistons sigh. Every morning my ex-adviser straps on snowshoes and clomps past our cabin on his way to the Institute, gliding atop the frozen crust like a Nordic vision of Jesus. I have given Alexandra an ultimatum: she has until commencement day to decide if she wants to marry me. If she does not want to marry me, I will pack my textbooks and electronic diagnostic equipment and move to Huntsville, Alabama.

When students jump off the Gehring building, they curse and scream as though their hands are on fire. I can't say I blame them. This is the set of words I use when I talk about the Institute: *hunger, numbness, fatigue, yearning, anger.* Old photographs of this town show a cathedral of pines standing in place of the bare quadrangle, and a sawmill on the Owahee in place of the nuclear plant. People in the pictures stare at the camera with an unmistakable air of melancholy, and looking at them I wonder if there was ever a happy season on this peninsula.

Alexandra tells me I'm ungenerous toward the Institute; she tells me the cold has freeze-dried my kindness. Here is a fact I cannot refute: on nights when the TechHotline is quiet and snow is settling in swells around the Gehring building, the silence is pure enough to make you want to weep. Windows in the Walsh Residence Hall blink off, one by one, until the quadrangle is lit only by moonlight. Icicles the size of children work loose and disappear into snowdrifts. Bark-colored hares hop lazily toward the Owahee. In the early-morning dark, before the sun climbs over the Gray building and the Institute begins to stretch, you can wade into a drift and lie back like an angel and let snow sift down onto you, and the only sound you hear is the slow churn of your own unwilling heart.

Slaney is the name of this town: a few thousand houses and shops crushed up against the Institute like groupies. Slaney has a short but tragic history: founded in 1906 by a Swede as a company town for the Michigan Land and Lumber Company;

within a year there were four hundred inhabitants, six board-inghouses, two general stores, a meat market, an icehouse, a whorehouse, seven saloons. The Swede, his heart full to bursting with pride, felled the tallest white pine in the county and propped it in the middle of Slaney's main drag as a monument to the town's greatness. By 1925 there was nothing left around Slaney except birch and tamarack and scrub poplar, and if tumbleweeds existed up here they'd have blown through the abandoned streets with a lonely rustle. The monumental white pine was dragged off to the sawmill in the middle of the night by timber thieves. The Swede drank himself into a stupor in Dan Gunn's empty saloon, then passed out during the twelve-block walk to his house and nearly froze to death.

That spring the hills hiccuped with dynamite blasts from prospectors looking for iron ore, and the state legislature chose Slaney as the location for the brand-new Michigan Engineering Institute. Every year in Slaney someone loses grip and commits an unspeakably self-destructive act. Here is something my ex-adviser does not think I know: seven years ago, when his ex-wife still lived in Slaney, he followed her to her house on Huron Street for eleven straight days, and one night as he crouched outside her kitchen window he was knocked unconscious by a blow from a policeman's nightstick. When he woke, he was shackled to a stainless-steel toilet. Ontonagon County, I've heard, has the toughest antistalking laws in the state.

On Friday nights the TechHotline is quiet. Dormitory windows are dark as graves, and the quadrangle echoes with shouts of horny undergraduates. I lock the TechInfo office, and Alexandra meets me on Mill Street outside the Caribou Lounge, where a six-piece band called Chicken Little plays Benny Goodman and Cab Calloway and Nat King Cole. Twenty-one-year-olds wearing circle skirts and two-tone shoes jam the dance floor and Charleston like they're scaring off demons. Rusty, the bandleader, wears a white silk suit and by eleven is drenched in sweat. I lindy until my knees ache, but Alexandra's just getting started: she climbs onto the stage and whispers into Rusty's ear. He says, *We're gonna do one for the spitfire in the pretty pink blouse.* I sit at the bar and watch Alexandra press up against strange men, and remind myself how miserable it was to be alone.

On Saturday nights students throng to the Newett Ice Arena to watch the hockey team lose to future NHLers from Houghton and Escanaba. Bartenders on Middle Street stockpile pint glasses and rub their hands together, waiting for the postgame crush. My ex-adviser locks his office door and drinks a half-bottle of sherry, then calls his ex-wife in Sturgeon Falls. He waits until she says *Hello? Who is this? John, please*—then hangs up. Afterward he dials the TechHotline, stammering, and I tell him to close his eyes and take a deep breath; I tell him everything will be all right. He says, *I'm sorry, Joseph, good Christ*, and begins to sniffle. Snow ambles down outside the TechInfo window. One Saturday, drunk, my ex-adviser called and managed to say, *Listen, I'm not going to repeat this: my daughter can be somewhat difficult, and I frankly don't know if you're up to the challenge.*

The Swede kept a leather-bound journal detailing the events of his life from the day he arrived in Slaney until the day he died, and I read a Xeroxed copy of it when the TechHotline is quiet. *Town has grown faster than even my most incautious estimates*, he wrote in 1911. *Andrew Street now one-quarter mile long. Irish, Finns, Cousin Jacks have come, and for some reason a band of Sicilians. No chicken for eight months.* When Slaney was booming in the 1910s, lumberjacks from as far as Bruce Crossing would descend on the town on weekends and get knee-walking drunk on Yellow Dog whiskey, then smash pub stools to splinters with their peaveys. Their steel-calked boots punched holes in Slaney's plank sidewalks. A tenderloin sprang up along the eastern edge of town, and the Swede met a young prostitute named Lotta Scott at Hugh Grogan's place on Thomas Street; she charged him two dollars. *Disarmingly frank*, he wrote. *Eyes dark as bituminous coal. Slim ankles. Short patience.*

Before I leave for the TechInfo office in the evening, Alexandra walks from room to room shedding her prim librarian's turtleneck and knee-length skirt and woolen tights, then lies back on the kitchen table, naked, ravenous. Her eyes follow my hands, nervous as squirrels, as I unbuckle myself. She tugs at the seam of my jeans. Outside, snow movers pound down the ice-packed street, their carbon-steel blades gouging the curb. Alexandra smells archival—glue and musty paper and indelible ink—and she loves sex as much as a snowman loves cold. This is what I do: I say a small prayer just before I begin, even though I am not religious. By her own count, Alexandra has had sex with more than thirty-five men.

Alexandra called the TechHotline one night and said, *Sometimes I wish you'd cool it a little bit, Joseph. I mean, I love you, I love all the nerdy things you do, I just don't understand why you feel the need to control me. We can love each other and still lead normal, semi-independent lives.* I could hear the soft rush of her breathing, a sound that made me dizzy. Alexandra is stingy with love; she is afraid of ending up like her parents, who squandered their love like drunks at a craps table. *I don't want to control you*, I explained. *I'm just a little uncomfortable with the idea of you having sex with strange men.*

The Swede in his journal described the deep silence of the woods, which seemed to him a cruel and beautiful sound. *Streets filled with sweet smell of pitch. Pine as far as I can see. Have fallen in love with that dissolute woman, Lotta Scott. Consumed by thoughts of her.* His spindly hand filled the journal pages. On May third he recorded the purchase of a new frock coat, for four dollars, tailored by *a clever Polander from Detroit*, and a set of linen *of surpassing quality*. Then on the tenth of May, 1919, the Swede in deliriously shaky script wrote that he and Lotta Scott were married in Burke's saloon by the justice of the peace with forty-four witnesses present. *I feel as the French explorers must have felt*, he wrote, *when they gazed for the first time upon the vast forests of this wondrous peninsula. Glorious, glorious chicken.*

I have tried to convince myself that Alexandra is not a tramp, that she simply suffers from too much love—that she loves too much for her own good. My ex-adviser knocks on the TechInfo door when he's too lonely to go home. One Saturday night, his shirt unbuttoned and a styrofoam cup of sherry balanced on his knee, he told me that I am too particular when it comes to love, that I should accept love no matter how it appears and be grateful. He sipped sherry in a languid, pensive manner. *There's a certain kind of imperfection that acts as a reference point, that gives a sense of perspective. Understand? The pockmark on the perfect cheek. The small, tragic flaw, like a beauty mark, but deeper.* He squinted out at the forlorn quadrangle. *I don't trust perfection. Alexandra's mother was so wonderfully, perfectly imperfect.* I once snuck into an auditorium in the

Gray building and watched my ex-adviser deliver a Physics 125 lecture on kinetic and potential energy. As he lectured, he smiled at a pair of sleepy-eyed sophomore girls, showing his artificially whitened teeth.

The harder I pull Alexandra toward me the harder she pushes away. It's heartbreaking. Every third Saturday in February the people of Slaney hold Winter Carnival, where they flood the Kmart parking lot and ice-skate under a mosaic of stars. Teenaged boys in Red Wings jerseys skate backward and play crack-the-whip to show off. My ex-adviser dons a black beret and circles the rink in long, fluid strides. Last February Alexandra and I skated couples, and in the chilly night her skin was as smooth and luminous as a glass of milk. *What a world!* I found myself thinking, *where a failed engineer with a crooked nose can skate couples with a syrup-haired woman who smells archival.* On Andrew Street we ate elephant ears and watched a muscular young townie lift people in his arms to guess their weight. Alexandra gave him a dollar, and he hoisted her up with one meaty arm and hugged her to his chest. Alexandra shouted *Whoa, hey! Wow!* and kicked her legs girlishly. When the townie put her down, she kissed him on the cheek, and when she came back and saw my face she said, *Oh, for God's sake, Joseph. Grow up.*

That night at three A.M. I turned on the bedroom light and knelt over Alexandra and asked her to be my wife. I felt tearful, exultant; I felt as vast and weightless as a raft of clouds; I felt all of Lake Superior welled inside my bursting chest. Sweat seeped from my trembling hands and dampened Alexandra's nightdress. *Joseph*, she said, *Joseph, Joseph, Joseph. Oh God.* She kissed my cheek, the same way she'd kissed the townie. *I just don't know, honey. I just don't know.*

This town: everywhere I look I see equations. Ice floes tumbling in the Owahee, snowflakes skidding past the TechInfo window: everywhere I look I see fractals and tensors and nonlinear differential equations. Some mornings when my TechInfo shift is over I stand in front of the Bradford Student Center and hand out pamphlets entitled "Proof of God's Existence by Series Expansion" and "The Combinatorics of Ancient Roman Orgies." Undergraduates walk broad circles around me. They're bundled in scarves and wool hats; only their eyes show. Alexandra tells me I make people uneasy, that not everything can be described by mathematics, and I tell her she's probably wrong.

I have considered admitting to Alexandra that I hate dancing but worry that she'll find another partner. One night at the Caribou Lounge I ducked out for fresh air, and on a whim wandered into the meager woods; there were no lights in sight, but the moonlit snow glowed bright enough to count change by. I lay down and stared up at the muddy streak of our galaxy. I thought—how to explain?—about the nature of imperfection. My ex-adviser every September stands before his Physics 125 class with his arms spread wide, like a preacher, and says, *Listen sharp, this is important: Nature. Hates. Perfection.* Alexandra says I sometimes remind her of her father, and this bothers her more than she can say.

In 1919 Slaney sent three million board-feet of pine down the Owahee, and the sawmill howled from morning to dusk. Lumberjacks, tired of two-dollar whores on Thomas Street, sent agonized letters to *Heart and Hand* matrimonial newspaper and convinced scared young women to pack their lives into trunks and board the train north. The Swede on May seventeenth—one week after his wedding—walked deep into the thinning woods and realized the pine would not last forever, that in four or five years it would be *cut out,* and Slaney would be *all caught up. Lumbermen will move westward, toward Ontonagon and Silver City,* he wrote. *Saloons will empty, sawmill will fall idle. Lotta departed for Hurley this morning at dawn to visit her mother. Declined my offer to accompany her.* Lotta Scott, before she left, borrowed two hundred dollars and a gold-plated pocket watch from the Swede.

I like my ex-adviser but worry that he cares too much about the wrong things. Larissa, the sophomore he bangs on Wednesdays in the Applied Optics Laboratory, has told him he'd better stop worrying about ancient history and start focusing on the here and now. *For Christ's sake,* my ex-adviser said, *she's nineteen years old—a child—telling me this. I love Larissa, but it's not the kind of love she thinks it is.* Alexandra does not remember the names of some of the men she has slept with. It was just sex, she explains, it wasn't a huge colossal thing. After the first time we made love, she stroked my hair and explained that I was not supposed to cry, that it was not supposed to be that way.

The tombstones in Slaney's cemetery have Finnish and Polish and Swedish names; they say COOPER and SAWYER and LUMBERMAN. Women who came to town, it seems, took a dismayed look around then headed back south. The lumberjacks died alone. The Swede, two weeks after Lotta left for Hurley, wrote, *Met a man Masters from Sault Ste. Marie, who claims the entire eastern half of the peninsula is cut out, not a stick of white pine standing. Martinville, Maynard, Bartlow he claims are empty, the houses deserted and mill torn down for scrap. Queer fellow. Says the land looks "naked and embarrassed" without the pine. No word from Lotta.*

The tenderloin was razed in a fit of prohibition righteousness in 1931 and lay vacant and weed-choked for twenty years. A Methodist church now stands where Dan Gunn's saloon used to be. Hugh Grogan's whorehouse has been replaced by an electronics store called Circuit Shack. The Swede wrote nothing in his journal for two weeks, then, *Took train to Hurley to find no trace of Lotta. Walked all up and down the dusty streets. Back in Slaney, heard from John Davidson that Lotta was seen on the Sault Ste. Marie train as far along as Allouez. Davidson was drunk and perhaps not being truthful. Nevertheless I fear she is gone completely.* This is a fact: I live with a woman with syrup-colored hair who loves me in a hard, unknowable way. My ex-adviser one Sunday in the TechInfo office, his feet propped on my desk and a cup of sherry balanced on his knee, smiled cryptically and said, *I believe I can solve your problem with my daughter. I have an idea. A theory.*

Alexandra left to visit her mother in Sturgeon Falls two weeks after Winter Carnival. At the station I blinked back a swell of longing as her train dragged slowly north. Alexandra leaned out the window and blew me a kiss, then tossed a small white bundle into the snow. She was supposed to stay one week in Sturgeon Falls; she was supposed to tell me *yes* or *no* when she returned. I searched for almost two hours but never did find the bundle she threw out the window.

My ex-adviser that night, sprawled in front of the TechInfo radiator like a housecat, told me I cannot expect to understand

Alexandra with mathematics alone, and that my view of love is analytical whereas his is romantic. My ex-adviser as he thawed smelled stale, like cooked cabbage. I set my mug of Seagrams down and on a wrinkled envelope wrote:

$$\frac{dJ}{dt} = \alpha J - \beta JA$$
$$\frac{dA}{dt} = \chi JA - \delta A$$

Where J *is my love,* A *is Alexandra's. The predator-prey equations— very elegant.* My words were cold clouds of Canadian whiskey. I rattled the ice cubes in my glass like dice. *You should trust mathematics,* I told him. *Nothing is too complex to describe with mathematics.* Alexandra called the next morning to tell me she'd decided to stay an extra week in Sturgeon Falls. I closed my eyes and listened to her syrup-colored voice. *I'm going to sit in my mother's sauna and think about everything. Have you ever been in a sauna, honey? It's incredible. First you feel like you're going to die, then you pass a certain point and feel like you're going to live forever.* She sighed. *And I'm helping my mother plan her wedding—she's getting remarried. Don't tell my father.*

I can build you a sauna. I can build it in the backyard, next to the big poplar.

His name is Harold. He breeds minks. There's hundreds of minks running around up here, honey. Her voice dropped to a whisper. *It makes me horny, in a weird way.*

I didn't say anything.

Joseph, I have never cheated on you, she said suddenly. Her voice held an edge of desperation. *I want you to understand that.* Alexandra, before she hung up, said that the bundle she threw out the train window contained a peach pit, nothing more.

My dissertation, which I never finished, was entitled *Nonlinear*

Control of Biomimetic Systems. The first chapter, which I finished, was entitled "On the Nature of Human Romantic Interaction." It begins: *Consider a third-order system with three states corresponding to three distinct people,* α, β, *and* χ. α *is attracted to both* β *and* χ. β *and* χ *are both attracted to* α *but not to each other. We would like to describe the behavior of this system over time.*

One night while Alexandra was in Sturgeon Falls, I sat staring into the darkened quadrangle for a long time. Finally I called her and said, *I can't wait forever. I can give you until commencement day, but then I'm moving to Huntsville, Alabama.* Alexandra was stunned, silent. *I don't know what else to do.* My ex-adviser convinced me to give Alexandra the Huntsville ultimatum. I had four handwritten pages of equations contradicting his advice, but he took the pencil from my hand and said, *Joseph, my friend, it's extremely simple: the only reason my daughter will not marry you is if she does not, in fact, love you.* Huntsville, Alabama. I chose Huntsville randomly off the map; I don't know what I'd do in a January without snow.

In my dissertation I proved analytically that it's possible to design a control system such that α's attraction to β grows exponentially, while α's attraction to χ diminishes exponentially. In the concluding paragraph, however, there is a caveat: *In practice the coupling factors are highly nonlinear and difficult to predict, and depend on phenomena such as shyness, boredom, desire, desperation, and self-knowledge, as well as numerous local conditions: the feeling of self-confidence gained from wearing a favorite pair of socks, the unexpected sorrow of seeing the season's first flock of geese flying south, etc.*

Alexandra returned from Sturgeon Falls five weeks before commencement day wearing a white muff, a gift from her mother's mink-breeder fiancé. She walked from the front door to the bedroom and dropped her suitcase on the bed, then walked back into the kitchen and gripped my shoulders and said, *Listen to me, Joseph: I love you. I love the shit out of you. But I'll never belong to you.*

That night I waited until Alexandra was asleep then pulled on boots and a parka and walked the half-mile to the Institute. The Gehring building was quiet except for a dull chorus of electronic devices. The TechInfo office was silent as a prayer. Suddenly I had an idea: I ran across the quadrangle to the Olssen building, the tallest building on campus, and sprinted from classroom to empty classroom, turning on lights. I formed a four-story lit-up A, then an L, then an E, then part of an X— then I ran out of classrooms. The Olssen building wasn't wide enough. Back in the TechInfo office, I threw open the window, breathless, and looked out across the quadrangle. ALE. The lights spelled ALE. A group of fraternity brothers had gathered, and when I appeared as a silhouette in the TechInfo window, they shouted, *Yo, hotline man! Ale! Fuckin' A!*

I closed the office door and turned off the lights, picked up the telephone and dialed. The phone rang three times, four times, five—and then Alexandra answered. Her voice was husky and irritable, the voice of a confident young woman disturbed from sleep. She said, *Hello? Who the hell is this—Joseph?*

I hung up.

They found ore in the hills around Slaney in 1926—not the glittery hematite they were seeing in Ishpeming, but a muddy blue sludge that assayed at sixty percent iron. Overnight, Slaney was reborn: the front glass of Dan Gunn's saloon was replaced and the floor replanked, Hugh Grogan's place on Thomas Street was scrubbed down and reopened. The Swede awoke from a month-long bender, his handwriting looser and less optimistic. *Strange to see trains unloading again. Excitement even at the meat market; ore, they say, is everywhere. No chicken for nine months.* My ex-adviser, one chilly April Sunday in the TechInfo office, explained that his ex-wife had taken out a restraining order, and if he called her one more time, he would be arrested. It took me two months to realize that *chicken* was the Swede's code word for intercourse.

Alexandra's mother, my ex-adviser said, *has the sort of posture you see in Victorian portraiture. Ivory skin, fingers that are almost impossibly delicate, yet strong. Beautifully strong, and that noble Victorian posture.* He stroked his stubbled chin and nodded, agreeing with himself. *And I treated her like shit on a heel.* My ex-adviser, one month before commencement day, somehow learned about his ex-wife's impending wedding, and he wandered into the quadrangle and slumped down in the dingy snow and refused to budge.

Alexandra was asked by her mother to be maid of honor. She sipped tea in the front room of our cabin, tearing pages from *Bride* magazine and acting like everything was okay. Alexandra does not understand the urgency that grips you at thirty; she does not understand the desperation that settles in at forty. I began staying late at work, wandering the Gehring building's damp subbasement tunnels. Down in the tunnels, I walked for hours without seeing a hint of the morning sky, and I felt how I imagined the old ore miners must have felt. One morning I told Alexandra that if she marries me, she does not necessarily have to stop seeing other men, and she looked at me with confusion and deep pity and slapped my face.

The Institute graduated its first class of engineers in 1930, but the residents of Slaney had no use for book-taught miners. The Swede, caught up in the excitement, paid thirty dollars for a claim on fifteen acres he'd never seen, and his first week out found a nugget of what he thought was solid gold. He squatted in the snow outside his lean-to and threw his head back and shouted at the moon. He was sixty-two years old. *As much as I can haul out*, he wrote. *Nuggets size of fists. Rapture.*

The Slaney Mountain was a wet hole of a mine with a safety record that made the sawmill look like a nursery. A 1931 cave-in sent pressurized air pounding through the shaft, and thirteen miners were punched off their feet then flung down, uninjured. A moment later the creaking support timbers fell silent, and a blanket of rock crushed the breath from their lungs. All thirteen died. In 1932 an Italian accidentally stubbed his cigar into a tub of freshly thawed dynamite, and the blast rattled windows as far away as Andrew Street. The Swede on March 13, 1933, convinced he'd hit a mother lode, sold his house and hocked his gold family ring for three hundred acres and a pair of mules. He sat all night atop his tiny hill, staring at the forest draped in darkness and dreaming of Pierce-Arrow automobiles and English leather gloves, and when the sun broke over the frozen valley he began to dig.

Two weeks before commencement day I woke to find Alexandra sitting at the foot of the bed, teary-eyed. *Bride* magazine lay tattered on her lap. She climbed beneath the comforter, sniffling, and said, *I wish you'd just quit what you're doing. I wish you'd let things keep going the way they're going.* It's crushing to remember the years before Alexandra: ordinary differential equations, cold beef pasties, the smell of melting solder and the heartless glow of a fluorescent lamp. I pulled Alexandra close and told her to close her eyes and take a deep breath, I told her everything would be all right, and she leaned her forehead against my chest and said *Cut it out.*

The Swede stockpiled gold for five months, then one morning hitched his mules to a rented sledge and paraded his mound of nuggets down Slaney's main drag. Old broken prospectors with hematite in their hair and an alcoholic's tremble stared out through Dan Gunn's front window and muttered softly at the sight. *Celebrated with sirloin steak and Yellow Dog whiskey, then strolled over to Thomas Street. Feasted on chicken.*

One week before commencement day the snow in the quadrangle began to shrink, then as if by sleight of hand the sun appeared where there had been only clouds. Physical plant workers tucked geraniums into planter boxes, and for the first time in months students unwrapped their scarves and looked around. One night I stayed sixteen hours at the TechInfo office. When I got home, I packed my books into milk crates and stacked them next to the door; Alexandra waited until I was asleep then unpacked them and placed them neatly back on the bookshelf. The nuggets the Swede had spent everything to pull from the ground were not pure gold, he discovered, but copper spiked with fatty veins of pyrite. The rock he'd spent five months hauling from his plot was worth nine dollars and sixty-three cents.

The morning before commencement day I purchased a non-refundable ticket to Huntsville. I had not showered, and the TechInfo office reflected what must be my own human smell: lemon and sour milk and powdered cumin. That night, his feet resting on the TechInfo desk, my ex-adviser said, *You should not let yourself go like this, Joseph. It's undignified.* After he left, two Slaney policemen knocked on the door. Their furry snow hats were pulled low on their foreheads. They were looking for my ex-adviser. When I asked what they wanted, the smaller policeman pursed his lips and said, *We can't divulge that information*. When I asked if my ex-adviser was in trouble, he said, *We can't divulge that information*.

The police, I learned eventually, were searching for a man who'd climbed into the heating ducts of the Benson dormitory and watched an unnamed freshwoman apply lotion to her calves. The police had swept the Gray building and sat for hours watching the student center, but no one had seen my ex-adviser. I told them I had no idea where he was. I told them it's not easy to hide in a town this small.

The ore around Slaney, it turned out, was not a single wide vein but pockety and impossible to follow. The D & C, Silver Lake, and Petersen mines stopped drilling in 1937. The Slaney Mountain mine—the first mine—stayed stubbornly open, and in 1939 engineers thought they'd hit a million-ton ore body. But two months later the ore was gone. The Mountain shut down. The last miners boarded the train west, for Houghton or Ishpeming. Dan Gunn nailed planks across the front window of his saloon and left Slaney for good. The Swede, penniless and without a home, took a bottle of Yellow Dog whiskey into the cut-out woods and sat down in the snow and put a .45 pistol in his mouth and pulled the trigger.

The pine around Slaney is gone. The ore is gone. The shaft house stands crumbling and windowless a half-mile from the Institute, and on Friday nights high-schoolers sneak inside and drink Boone's Farm Strawberry Hill and grope one another. My ex-adviser says that men never dig for iron or copper or coal; secretly, in their heart's heart, they're digging for gold. The Swede before he shot himself in 1940 wrote: *Heard from a man Jonsson that Lotta is in Grand Rapids and married to a furniture magnate. Said he saw them two months ago in church, Lotta dressed in silk and singing a beautiful soprano. Not certain Jonsson was being truthful; told of Lotta only after securing a loan of thirty dollars. So be it. Wherever Lotta is I wish her happiness. I write these words without regret.*

On the morning of commencement day the air smelled salty, like trouble, and from nowhere a milk-gray sheet fell over the sky and the temperature dropped twenty degrees in twenty minutes. By eight A.M. snow was swirling in the late May breeze, and by nine there were four inches on the highway and the radio was saying it looked like we were going to get socked but good. Alexandra and I stayed in bed. I rolled her into a position we called the log drive, and she told me—she shouted—that she loves me, goddammit, *yes*, and wants to be with me forever. I stopped. Outside, the wind sobbed. Alexandra, her face flushed the color of ripe rhubarb, stumbled from the bedroom and closed the door. Forty minutes later, when it was clear she wasn't coming back, I bundled myself in a parka and thermal snow pants and set off for the Institute.

From outside the TechInfo office I heard a floorboard creak, then a moist sniffle. I opened the door: Alexandra was sitting in the TechHotline chair in front of the window, staring into the quadrangle. She looked at me; she looked back out the window; she shrugged awkwardly and said, *So, this is it. The famous office.*

In the quadrangle a stage had been erected near the Gray building, and on the lawn an assembly of crimson-gowned seniors squirmed and hooted in the driving snow. Behind them, underdressed parents shivered in their seats, wondering what kind of people could live in a place like this. At the edge of the quadrangle the Caribou Brass Band sent up a frozen-lipped Sousa march. I drew the window shade, momentarily nostalgic at the sight of so much unbridled optimism, and as I did the crowd quieted and the provost took the podium and cleared her throat. *Students, parents, distinguished guests, fellow alumni and alumnae: welcome. Today is a joyous day.*

Alexandra took the telephone from my desk and placed it on the bookshelf. She scooted onto the desk, her snow-booted feet not touching the floor, and pulled me down to her. *Just lie here,* she said. *Don't get funny.* Her breathing was loud in my ear: a seashore, a multitude. I kissed her smooth neck, and let myself believe for a moment that we were two strangers pressed together, shivering with possibility. Alexandra stroked my back, but when I began to stir, she gripped my shoulders with heartbreaking finality. *Just don't,* she said. *Okay? Please. Just stay.*

From the quadrangle the voice of the Institute's first female graduate drifted into the office. *I remember a bedroom was made up for me in the infirmary, and boys would stand outside arguing over who would walk me to chemistry class. I remember walking to class wondering how in the world a girl like myself ended up at a place with so many wonderful, wonderful boys.* Alexandra shifted beneath me. Suddenly there was a ripple of applause, and the microphone reverberated as if it had been dropped, then the tinny, shouted voice of my ex-adviser announced that he was having an immoral relationship with an undergraduate.

Alexandra struggled to her feet. The crowd hushed. Alexandra shoved aside the window shade and said, *Jesus Christ, fuck, Dad*—then grabbed her parka and threw open the TechInfo door and clattered down the Gehring building stairs.

Outside, the crowd had fractured into a jumble of bewildered voices. The provost stood at the podium with her arms raised, saying, *Okay, let's just be calm, people*— Then a woman screamed and two people stood and pointed: I followed their gaze to the roof of the Gray building, where my ex-adviser stood in full academic regalia, looking like an Arthurian pimp. His arms were hugged against his chest in a way that struck me as tremendously fragile. He shifted his weight from foot to foot, his crimson robes billowing in the snowy breeze; then I spotted Alexandra, a red-jacketed streak across the quadrangle. She sprinted past the confused brass band, past the podium, and burst through the Gray building's tall front doors.

I threw open the window, half-expecting the TechHotline to ring, as a distant wail went up from the Slaney firehouse. Atop the Gray building my ex-adviser was a blot against the chalky sky, a singularity. He tugged off his eight-cornered hat and tossed it limply over the edge. It fluttered down, down, down, then landed on the sidewalk, flopped once, and lay flat. An anxious moan rose from the crowd. He climbed the safety railing and leaned over the roof edge, his wispy hair whipping in the breeze, and the provost over the loudspeaker said, *Okay, okay, wait: Jesus God*.

Then Alexandra appeared behind her father. She approached him slowly. He turned to her and spread his arms wide, his face a mask of nervous relief, then seemed to slip on the icy roof: he took a quick step backward and froze, arms thrown up to heaven, and then he was airborne. Down he went, his crimson robes rippling as he bicycled in the frozen air then disappeared without a sound into a steep bank of snow.

A chorus of screams rose up, and the provost whispered *Sweet Jesus* into the microphone and turned away from the roof and covered her face. Alexandra rushed to the roof edge. A quartet of Slaney firemen jogged into the courtyard with a folded-up safety net and looked around, confused. I made a quick calculation: a 180-pound man, falling thirty feet under an acceleration of 32.2 feet per second squared—I drew the shade and turned away from the window and closed my eyes.

Wind howled past the TechInfo window. A baby broke into a restless wail. After what seemed like a long time I heard a hopeful shout, and I peeked around the shade: my ex-adviser was struggling from the snowbank, clutching his left shoulder, surrounded by shocked firemen. I closed my eyes. I looked again: Alexandra, red parka gone and hair whipped into a cloud, rushed hip-deep into the snowbank and threw her arms around her father's neck. She touched his cheek, as if to make sure he was real and not some snow-blown mirage. My ex-adviser, his eyes squeezed shut with pain, slumped down in the drifting snow and hugged his daughter with his good arm and began to weep.

The Detroit train left at eleven-thirteen P.M., and from there it was two connections and twenty-one hours to Huntsville. I sat in the TechInfo office until it was time to leave for the station, and when the TechHotline rang, I didn't pick up. The CALL light threw jagged shadows against the dark office walls. I knew there were equations describing the contour of the shadows, the luminescent intensity of the CALL light, the heat distribution in my hands as I clasped them together, the stress distribution in my eyelids as I pressed my eyes shut. In the quadrangle, snow drifted down with perfect indifferent randomness. In thousands of dormitory bedrooms, young men and women were asleep and dreaming of numbers.

I would begin a new line of research in Alabama, I decided.

I would throw away my textbooks and Institute notepads and start fresh. What effect does geography have on love? What effect does weather have on love? There are events in nature, I've noticed, that cannot be explained or reproduced, that simply *are*. It's enough to give a person hope.

THE PHRENOLOGIST'S DREAM

I.

THAT morning he rose at sunrise and stepped into trousers and brogues in the tea-colored light. The room had no washbasin, so he wiped his face on his shirttails and ran a finger along his gluey front teeth. On the side table lay a bottle of hair tonic, a pair of white satin gloves, and a scatter of coins that he counted by feel as he dropped them into his vest pocket: ten dollars, five and a half cents. Although the sum was considerable, Jeremiah felt a shade of disappointment: twenty-four examinations, half of them women, and not a single skull had quickened his heart.

He stepped out into a windless day barbed with cold. He nipped at a pint bottle of whiskey while a sleepy groom hitched his buggy, then he patted his horse's mane and climbed aboard, and with a shake of the reins started down the empty road. New Buffalo: two streets wide by six long, a flyspeck on the map. He rolled past a print shop and Methodist church and tinsmith's, and was nearing a squat brick bank when he saw the girl, standing on the sidewalk with a valise at her feet, waving at Jeremiah as if he should stop.

He reined the horse and watched her tramp across the muddy road. She stopped beside the buggy and looked up. "I'd like to ride with you. Please."

Her arms were folded brazenly across her chest, but her high forehead and watery blue eyes made her seem sweet and young, like a child dressed in a woman's clothing. Her brow was marked by a frayed white scar. Her hair hung in lusterless brown braids, flecked with sand and bits of thistle, as though they'd been dragged through weeds. He said, "My apologies, I don't believe I know you."

"You examined me yesterday," she said. "I have excellent veneration and friendship, and I'm endowed with superior intuition as to truth. You said my mental temperament is highly developed. My name's Sarah Bennet."

"Miss, I examined twenty-four people yesterday. I didn't invite any of them to travel with me."

The girl held his gaze but said nothing.

"You don't even know where I'm headed!"

"I need to get to Detroit, but anywhere north is fine." She frowned. "I can't pay anything. I had my bag stolen last week by a Negro."

A wheat-brown dog limped toward them along the gutter, then paused to nose through a knob of food scraps. "I'm sorry about your bag. Now, if you wouldn't mind."

Jeremiah nudged the horse forward a few paces. The girl didn't move. Now he remembered: the braids were a wig, which had shifted beneath his fingers during her examination.

Besides having a hairless head, the girl had no eyebrows or eye-lashes, no pale downy fuzz on her cheek. Her skin was smooth, glossy, like a newly glazed bowl. It was a shame: save for the missing hair, she was a fair-looking girl.

"My husband's sick with fever in Detroit," she shouted. "If you were a damn gentleman you'd offer me a ride. I'll say noth-ing more."

Her voice held a hint of despair, and evoked for Jeremiah his previous night's ramble through New Buffalo's streets, drunk on apple brandy, searching for a reddish light glowing in an up-stairs window. But there were only stray dogs and dark shop-fronts and his own hollow footsteps. He'd slumped against a lamppost to stop the street's spinning. Some damn town, he thought, where a man can't buy a night's companionship. Then the walk back to the boardinghouse, fists stuffed in his pockets and greatcoat billowing in the chilly breeze. Laughter rose from shadows and doors slammed and music burst from open saloon windows, each sound the reflection of another person.

Jeremiah shivered, and licked his lips. He said, "Step up."

They drove north from New Buffalo on a rutted turnpike, Jeremiah working the reins with one hand while he listened to the girl talk: about her husband's skill as a squirrel hunter, about her unfailingly good health, about a sermon on the evils of Catholicism. The buggy rattled and jounced, its thorough-braces creaking; it felt like they were riding on a pathway of ribs. Near noon they passed into a meadow ridged by maples, the trees' scarlet leaves blazing, and for a while the girl fell silent. Then she shifted in her seat and let out a loud sigh.

"This road might be pleasant if it had some gravel. I traveled once from Colson to Dayton. Feared my teeth would shake loose, the ride was so rough."

"At least the view is agreeable enough," Jeremiah said. "Most of Ohio is plain dull. Drive long enough with a miserable view, it works on your mind."

"My husband says the view in this country is everywhere the same: a horse's backside."

Jeremiah chuckled, and glanced sideways at the girl to measure her seriousness. She was older than he'd first supposed: from the creases on her hands and faint weathering around her eyes, he guessed she might be twenty-five. She rode with her shawl unbuttoned in the September chill.

"Do you mind if I ask how you lost your hair?"

"Never had any. It's my unique burden to bear." She squinted at Jeremiah. "My head must be an open book to you, right? You needn't have bothered with touching, when you examined me. I should've just yanked off my wig."

"I've examined plenty of bald men," Jeremiah said. "The lack of hair gives me keener insight into their character."

She snorted. "You told me a load of bunkum. Said I was skilled with numbers, but I'm not. Said I had a strong predilection for poetry, but I don't care a damn."

"Watch your tongue. You shouldn't criticize what you don't understand."

The girl rolled her eyes, staring at the road ahead.

He thought back to her examination: her skull had showed well-formed veneration and wit, but feeble amativeness, adhesiveness, and conjugality; it was the skull of a barmaid, or washwoman. No wonder she was unhappy with her assessment. But Jeremiah had his own doubts about phrenology, which he probed and worried like loose teeth. If a man's skull was injured through accident, would his temperament necessarily change? If his skull showed a faculty for stealing or telling falsehoods, was he predestined to be a thief or liar? The questions troubled him, and though he'd pondered them for hours, he'd never reached a single satisfying conclusion. Jeremiah's own skull suggested skill in language and memory, strong benevolence and friendship—things he knew to be false—and mediocre intelligence. So who was he? The clever, reticent man he saw in himself, or the dense, generous man his skull claimed?

"Personally, I consider myself an excellent judge of character," the girl continued. "I don't need to rub a man's head, I can gauge him a mile away."

"Do you mind if I ask how you gauge me?"

"Well, you've a streak of kindness, I know that firsthand, and it's plain that you're a smart fellow. Seems to me, though, that you possess an unhealthy amount of gloom."

A blush spread over Jeremiah's neck. "What about yourself? I hope you'll share your insights into your own character."

"It's just like you said: I have excellent veneration and friendship. All the best qualities." She laughed, a musical giggle. "My goodness, I'm just a silly woman. You should forget everything I've said."

Jeremiah said, "I already have."

A breeze rose as the buggy's shadow faded into dusk. He wrapped a scarf around his chin and flicked his horse to a trot, and just before the road disappeared in darkness they saw the inn: a two-story house beside a dozen rows of apple trees, anchoring the edge of a cornfield.

Jeremiah paid the proprietor sixty cents for two rooms, then followed the girl up a narrow stair, the oak planks creaking beneath their feet. In his room he dropped his trunk in the corner then listened at the door: he heard the girl's tread soften then stop; then a door scraped open and shut.

He leaned close to the bureau's cracked mirror, the contours of his face discouragingly familiar. Jeremiah's skin was coated with dust, and when he rubbed his forehead it felt brittle and smooth, like parched clay. He opened his case and withdrew a pint bottle of whiskey. Just take a damn breath, he told himself. Open the damn door. He wished he had a bouquet of wildflowers.

He stood motionless for a long time, listening to the gusting wind, then paced down the hallway and tapped on the girl's door. It eased open. She was standing at the window, her bonnet untied and wig aslant, her valise open on the bed. "It's okay," she said. "You can come in."

Jeremiah's heart seemed to slow, as though it were pumping molasses. He moved behind the girl, and when he touched her shoulder, she flinched as though she'd been stung. "I'm nervous," she said, "I'm sorry. I'm not accustomed to travel. I think it's unbalanced my mood."

Jeremiah tilted the bottle toward her, but she shook her head. He swallowed a long gulp. "Great God in heaven," he gasped, "this is rough stuff." He took another pull.

"Tell me something about yourself," the girl said. "Anything. Tell me your mother's name."

"Lettice."

"Tell me where your father was born."

"Albany, New York." Her dress had shifted, and an arc of skin glowed white at the base of her windburned neck. Jeremiah moved toward her, but she stepped to the door. She seemed both bold and frightened, like a cat confronting a strange animal.

He said, "You say your husband's in Detroit, then? Seems an unusual arrangement."

"My husband's an unusual man. He used to take my hair and pitch it onto the roof, when he got angry. I'd wait until he fell asleep then fetch it with a ladder. Sometimes the crows got it first."

Jeremiah was silent for a moment. "What'll you do when you find him?"

"Kiss him to death or shoot him. I don't know which." She took the whiskey bottle and sipped, grimacing. "This isn't a regular occurrence for me. I want you to understand that." Then she slid the wig from her head and tossed it onto the bed.

A hot shock scalded Jeremiah. Sweat gleamed on the girl's bare scalp, the skin silky and pale, as though it had never seen sun. She smoothed her palms over her head, then unknotted her dress and rolled her shoulders back, and let the clothes slide to her ankles. The girl glanced at him, her cheeks flushed with shame. Jeremiah lowered his eyes. His stomach trembled near sickness. He heard a hush of settling underclothes, then the mattress'd stiff rustle. She said, "All right, Mr. Simon. Now," and touched his fingers.

He whispered, "Great God in heaven."

He'd dreamed she would be beautiful, the girl with the perfect skull. In his dreams she wore a blue satin frock with a burgundy shawl, or a pink silk pelisse, or a white crinoline. Her hair fell in tight blond ringlets or was swept into an auburn chignon. Her eyes were hazel or cornflower blue or gray. Some mornings Jeremiah woke in a sweat, stirred by an ache that nothing would calm except his own shameful hand; others he woke to a bitter tang that he understood to be the taste of loneliness. He was twenty-nine and had been on the road for seven years, and had come to hate the countryside and its gorgeous emptiness.

Albany, Franklin, Harrisburg, Clear Lake, Staunton, Sherwood Crossing, Morehead, Russell: he'd driven from New York all through Pennsylvania, down into Virginia and Kentucky, now up into the endless forest of Ohio. Every morning he donned white satin gloves with pearl buttons at the wrists, and by noon they were spotted with dirt and macassar oil and crushed lice. In his vest pocket Jeremiah carried a leather-bound book; for each woman he examined, he penned three numbers: their amativeness, adhesiveness, and conjugality, rated from one to seven. At night in the hotel room, he wrung his gloves in the washbasin, then leafed through page after page of data, the figures as varied and perplexing as women themselves.

Nagle had shown that skull size was determined by race; Layfield had proven the relationship between combativeness and climate. Jeremiah had first read their monographs by the glow of a tallow stub, in his father's home in Albany. He was a boy of twenty-two—a man, supposedly—with awkward manners and long, dirty hair; he'd never courted a girl, never kissed a girl goodnight. He was thrilled by phrenology's brash wisdom—for what was science's greatest purpose, if not to explain man to himself? As he read, he gingerly touched his own skull, propping the book open with his elbows. Surely, he reasoned, a woman's capacity for love couldn't be random.

It must be related to her devoutness, Jeremiah thought, or education, or father's occupation—something. A notion coagulated in his mind, then one morning presented itself whole, like a fresh white egg: that a woman's capacity for love was revealed as the sum of her amativeness, adhesiveness, and conjugality. He'd jerked out of bed and struggled into clothes, then raced across the empty fields to the print shop. He'd purchased texts by Fowler and Gall, and a small leather-bound book, the pages as blank and clean as new snow.

He'd set off that next Monday, stopping first in Buffalo then following the turnpike south, his book pages filling with numbers. He grew whiskers, to appear more mature, but his appearance in the mirror was that of a grim stranger. He shaved his chin clean. That December, in Scranton, he began a monograph entitled *The Amorous Organs of Respectable American Women*. He wrote ten pages then tore them into strips.

His sentences were knots. His data were as formless as soup. His examination method was correct, surely, but perhaps his judgment of organ size was inconsistent, or he was misinterpreting the results? The only noteworthy measurements, for some reason, seemed to come from the skulls of prostitutes. At night Jeremiah lay awake, in rooms whose shabbiness never ceased to dishearten him. A scientist's life, he thought miserably, was like a midnight walk across an unfamiliar field, without a lantern, without even the moon's faint glow for guidance.

A year passed and then another. In Hopewell he rewrote the monograph's introduction, but though he pored over ninety pages of data, he couldn't prove a single hypothesis. One morning in Louisville he woke with a start. It was his birthday—the realization struck him as a cold joke. For what had he accomplished in the past years, besides touring small, worthless towns? He was no longer young but wasn't yet wise; he'd developed a theory of love but had never been loved; he'd read much but understood, it seemed, very little. And lately those dreams of beautiful women, which felt like a taunt from his sleeping self. They left him lonely but with an ember of hope: in his dreams he found the girl with the perfect skull, courted her, and made her his wife.

He woke to a rap on the door and a flood of sunlight that caused his forehead to twinge in pain. The rap repeated, followed by a woman's muffled voice: "Open up, please. Need to tidy the room."

Jeremiah rolled onto his elbow, feeling a familiar dull confusion. Then he realized: he was in the girl's room, Sarah Bennet's. Sunlight poured through filmy curtains and showed the baseboards and floor to be speckled brown with tobacco juice. He pulled on his trousers and patted the pockets: coins, watch, a fold of banknotes. On the floor beside the bed stood a half-empty bottle of whiskey. The girl's valise was nowhere to be seen.

He hurried down the hallway to his own room: the bed was undisturbed, and in the corner near the window sat his closed trunk. His skull case was gone. Jeremiah circled the bed, then lifted the quilt and peered beneath the frame. His felt-lined case, with his Fowler and Gall texts, his handbills, his porcelain demonstration skulls—he strode back to the girl's room and looked beneath the bed. The case was gone.

"Damn it to hell," he hissed, and kicked the doorframe. His forehead felt squeezed, as though his perceptive organs were constricting, and Jeremiah rubbed his temples, but that only sharpened the pain. Downstairs, the proprietor sat in a rocker beside a cold fireplace, reading a newspaper. "Excuse me, sir: the bald girl I was with, did she leave?"

The proprietor was a tall, weary-looking man with thread-worn trousers and a shabby chin beard. He stared at Jeremiah over his newspaper. "She wasn't bald at all."

"She was, she wore a wig. I believe she stole my skulls." Jeremiah's voice had risen to a strained pitch. "Did a stage pass here?"

The man nodded. "Came last night, but didn't stop long. Toward Mentonville."

Jeremiah tried to focus his thoughts, but his head felt as though it were filled with fog. The proprietor said, "How is it she stole your skull?"

"Skulls. They're scientific articles," Jeremiah said. "They're valuable. I'm a phrenologist."

The proprietor set the newspaper in his lap and scrutinized Jeremiah. With his sleep-creased shirt and tousled hair, Jeremiah reckoned he was a pitiful sight. "I'd like to hear my future," the man said. "I'll pay ten cents."

"I don't have time, I'm sorry." Jeremiah took up his coat and trunk, then stopped at the door. "And even if I did, I wouldn't work for a damn dime."

Outside, he hitched his buggy while the proprietor watched from the doorway. "To Mentonville," the man said, pointing with his newspaper along the only road in sight. "Straight as a loon's leg."

Jeremiah snapped the reins, and the buggy jolted forward. He felt vaguely ashamed, as though he'd misunderstood some simple fact. He tried to clear his mind, but every stray thought led to the previous night's clouded moon, the gossipy whisper of cornstalks, the girl's taut voice. Her pliant skin, the tight clench of her fist. The smooth scar on her brow.

He glanced back and saw the proprietor in the distance,

standing in the road. The man raised a hand, but Jeremiah didn't return the farewell. *I'd like to hear my future,* he'd said, but Jeremiah knew he could no more tell the man his future than he could tell his own.

II.

In October Jeremiah traded his buggy for a worn mud wagon and seventy dollars coin. He was broke: in Mentonville and Carlow he'd examined only a dozen people. On the morning of his departure from Carlow he'd learned that a Baptist circuit rider had spoken out against phrenology, calling it quackery and an enemy of Christian religion. Jeremiah earned only enough money to pay for his meals.

He drove to Essex, where he examined a printer and his daughters in exchange for a run of simple handbills: MR. J. SIMON, PRACTICAL PHRENOLOGIST. He wrote, *will be examining Men, Women, and Children at the Wayne Hotel until Thursday, October 12.* He meandered along the town's streets, posting bills and knocking at every boardinghouse door, to ask if they'd seen a chestnut-haired girl with no eyebrows. Always the answer was no.

He worked three days in Essex, but the fourth morning walked past the Wayne Hotel and took a seat in the back corner of John Sullivan's saloon. He drank glass after glass of flip, until he'd achieved a superb, shimmering calm. *My dear little whore of a wife has run off with Indian fighters,* he repeated, to a man drinking at the next table, until the barkeep rapped his knuckles against the wall. Jeremiah dropped a dollar on the floor and staggered into the street and started toward a lit-up house with piano music trickling from an open window.

A squat, rouged woman with rotten front teeth opened the

door. "You must be here for a dance," she said, ushering Jeremiah inside. In the corner of the parlor, an old black woman played "Oh! Susanna" on a battered upright.

The upstairs bedroom smelled of lavender and urine and sour tobacco juice. "Regular is one dollar," the woman said. "Anything else costs extra." She shucked her black dress and pantaletts into a heap. Her chest and waist and hips were a single fleshy trunk, her breasts like a pair of stones dropped in silk stockings.

"Regular is fine," Jeremiah said. "I thank you, miss."

"My name's Constance." She scooted onto the bed and let her legs fall open. "Please try not to muss my hair."

Jeremiah unbuttoned his trousers and climbed atop the woman, in his drunken state feeling like a passenger on a gently rolling barge. The bedframe groaned. A hot urge burned in his stomach, as though he'd swallowed a shovelful of embers; he shut his eyes and grasped the woman's head, his fingers tracing her sentiments then falling to her propensities. She could make a decent mother, he thought, or nursemaid. A decent wife. Good lord.

"Quit." She yanked his hands down to her shoulders. "My hair."

He woke the next morning with a rheumy cough. He drove to Andrew and stepped out to post handbills, then returned to the hotel and sank into bed. That night he lay in a feverish sweat, paging through Fowler's *Life, Its Factors and Improvement:*

Man, know thyself! In this work is contained a study of the mental fountains from which all feelings and actions emanate, being an unequalled personal benefaction none can afford to ignore.

The passage's haughty assurance raised a prickle of annoyance in Jeremiah. He opened his leather-bound book, the first time in months, and read a neatly penned paragraph:

All men are desirous of attracting a devoted, affectionate, and amorous woman, as decreed by Nature's supreme law. Not all women, however, are equally capable of providing suitable affection, due to poorly developed organs of amativeness, adhesiveness, and conjugality. From observations made by the Author during his extensive travels, we can draw several conclusions, first regarding

The sentence ended as an empty page. He leafed forward, and before him were data from New Buffalo, Ohio. Somewhere in the swarm of numbers was his appraisal of the girl.

He'd seen her often in the past weeks: in the morning as he stropped his razor, in the evening as he wrung dingy water from his satin gloves. *Sarah Bennet:* the name roused him, like a curse. He tried to push his feelings toward anger, but instead his mind lingered on her musical giggle, her whiskey-scented breath, her downcast eyes as her dress crumpled to the floor. Her scarred, delicate brow, her hairless scalp. The memories were obscene, thrilling. She's no one, Jeremiah told himself, just a strumpet and damn thief, with a skull as ordinary as a peddler's. But when he thought about her, his loneliness disappeared, like hunger after a rich meal.

The next morning he sat in his wagon at the northern edge of Andrew. Blue fingerboards pointed toward Carrier and Gultin's Prairie, both names dimly familiar, as though he might've passed through a month or year ago. A porter lazed on the sidewalk, spitting tobacco juice at a flat stone. Jeremiah waved to him and pointed toward the northwest road. "Can you tell me where it leads?"

"Carrier, then on to Rose." He wiped his moist lips. "Further along it forks toward Detroit, I believe."

"You don't know for certain?"

The man shrugged. "Never been north of Rose. Never had reason."

Clouds had gathered in a gray raft, and now a few snow-flakes settled with a sting on Jeremiah's freshly shaved cheeks. He turned up his collar and nodded at the porter, and with a shake of the reins started slowly northwest.

He drove into Carrier in late afternoon, the sun a low yolk and a crisp breeze feathering the roadside sedge. Gigs and spring wagons rattled past; a boy ambled down the sidewalk, amid a bustle of men and women, shouting *Apples! Fresh apples here!* Windows caught the sun and glowed orange, like the eyes of night-time animals. Jeremiah stopped outside a hotel and stepped down, his legs wobbly and sore, as though he'd been in rough seas. He was hoisting his trunk onto the sidewalk when he saw the handbill, tacked to an announcement board: MR. J. SIMON, PRACTICAL PHRENOLOGIST.

He let the trunk topple onto its side. *The Public is respectfully informed of the presence of Mr. J. Simon, Phrenologist and Physiognomist, at the Three Flags Hotel, from October 24–27.* He didn't read further; he'd composed the words himself and could recite them from memory. The location and dates were penned in a cramped, childish script. He pulled the notice from the board and held it in both hands. *See also the Living Phrenological Diagram, an Extraordinary and Wonderful Curiosity.* Jeremiah slipped the handbill into his vest pocket, then stopped a news vendor and asked directions to the Three Flags Hotel.

A note was tacked beside the hotel door: *Mr. J. Simon is ill and not available for examinations. See the Living Phrenological Diagram, Admn. 25 cents.* He stepped into an open foyer and a loose knot of men and women. Across the room, standing behind a low table, was Sarah Bennet.

She was wearing a black cotton dress and black satin gloves but no bonnet or wig: her scalp looked like a spider's web or an old, cracked mirror. Jeremiah froze. Her head was crisscrossed with thin black lines that divided her skull into its thirty-five organs, combativeness and wonder and acquisitiveness and wit sectioned into neat parcels. Jeremiah's porcelain skulls sat before her on the table—a white laborer, a Chippewa Indian, and an African—and she looked like one of the skulls come to life, something from a dream or nightmare. Beside Jeremiah, a boy clutched his mother's skirts, crying, his eyes fixed on the girl's painted scalp.

Jeremiah jostled through the crowd. The girl was talking to a man in a dirty pea jacket, gesturing toward his perceptive organs. Her gaze flicked to Jeremiah. She smiled at the man; then a scarlet flush spread over her face. She turned to Jeremiah and attempted a smile. "Please don't cause a fuss," she whispered. "I apologize sincerely."

"I can't decide whether to get the police," Jeremiah said, "or whip you myself. Or both."

Sweat glazed her painted forehead, but she maintained a fierce grin. "I'll pay for the skulls and handbills, I promise. Please, keep your voice low. I beg of you."

"You rob me, then tell me to keep quiet?" Jeremiah's voice rose to a shout. "And your skull—you painted the organs wrong, do you know that? Do you know your head frightens children?"

"I was ill that night," she said quickly. "My stomach. I woke and thought—I feared my insides were falling out. Like some-one was shoving a hot poker into me, then twisting it back out. There was some blood. I needed a doctor."

Her voice was hoarse with fear, and what sounded like sin-cerity. "Then you should have woken me. I would have brought you to a doctor."

She motioned to the crown of Jeremiah's skull, his organ of veneration, as though she were responding to a polite question. "I was angry at you, for making me feel so terrible. So I left."

"But first you took my case. Why didn't you steal my damn buggy, while you were at it?"

She stared at Jeremiah, her mouth set in a thin line.

"And what about your dear sick husband? Have you been to Detroit and back?"

"That was no lie. I'm headed to Detroit." She pressed her satin-gloved fingers against Jeremiah's temples. "Let me finish with these people, please. They paid twenty-five cents apiece."

Her touch brought a rush of angry heat and a deep, liquid tugging. He jerked his head away. "And you, pretending to understand phrenology, for land's sake. Taking money from these poor people, giving them nothing but a spectacle and some lies. It's an offense against science." He turned to the hushed crowd. "This woman's a charlatan and a damn fraud!"

"I *know* you, Mr. Simon." She took his hand, and when he tried to pull away she gripped it urgently. "You're patient and thoughtful. You possess profound compassion."

"You should pray that I do," Jeremiah said.

He found a saloon across the street from the hotel and drank brandy at the front window as the afternoon darkened. The girl appeared on the sidewalk at dusk, hugging the skull case to her chest. She wore a black bonnet to match her dress and gloves; to Jeremiah she looked like an engraving he'd once seen of a restless soul in limbo. He watched her with inebriated patience.

You possess an unhealthy amount of gloom, she'd told him, that morning on the road from New Buffalo. Jeremiah knew she was right: even now he felt shadowed in melancholy, as though any effort he might make would end in failure. Science, he knew, was full of failure—failed hypotheses, failed experiments, failed theories—and the thought occurred to him that he should quit phrenology. I could sell my books, he thought, become a printer or carpenter, something simple. How could he ever predict a woman's capacity for love? The question was too immense; better to leave it to true scientists, like Wells and Fowler. He watched the girl step inside a shabby hotel, then Jeremiah licked the last drops from his glass and hauled himself to his feet.

He listened outside her door: silence; a muffled cough. He turned the knob, and the door swung inward. She was standing at the basin, wiping black smudges from her scalp. Jeremiah's skull case lay beneath the window.

He said, "How'd you enjoy pretending to be my assistant?"

She chuckled, without looking at him. "Wasn't much of a prize. Lousy beds and too many miles in those damn coaches. Felt like my jaw would rattle off its hinges."

"That's rich. You rob a man, then complain about the comfort of your escape." He watched her scrutinize her reflection in a hand mirror. "You sound like a woman who doesn't have many worries."

"If you meant to do something, I reckon you'd have done it already." She took her wig from the bedpost and settled it on her head. She stared evenly at Jeremiah.

"You're a fool girl. You should be worried I'm going to have you in jail, or run out of town. I could do either of those things in a moment."

She clasped her hands but said nothing.

Jeremiah stuffed his fists in his pockets to hide their trembling. He wished he had a glass of whiskey. "This entire situation is crazy. Those poor coots can't see that you don't know two cents about phrenology?"

"I read the silly books; I invent what I can't remember. I don't give a fart in a whirlwind for phrenology."

"Well," Jeremiah said, "this entire situation is crazy."

The girl's wig had been brushed to a gloss, and her cheeks were daubed reddish-brown; as Jeremiah stared, a faint grin grew on her lips. The sight pushed the breath from him.

"I must admit," she said, "I enjoy the dramatics—it makes me feel like a theater actress. I'll pay for the skulls."

"I'm planning to take them back, thank you."

"You don't seem to want them. If you did, you'd have replaced them by now."

She's right, Jeremiah thought. I could have bought plaster skulls in Andrew. "Two hundred dollars. They're porcelain, from London."

She tried unsuccessfully to hide her surprise. "I'll give you forty dollars."

"I reckoned as much." He hefted the skull case.

The girl's gaze followed the case, then rose anxiously to Jeremiah. A notion that had been lingering on the margins of his mind suddenly presented itself. "Maybe I will let you buy them." He set the case down and rubbed his jaw, feigning indifference. "Maybe I'll keep you in reach until you can pay the two hundred."

"How do you plan to keep me in reach?"

He paced to the dresser and took up the room key, then locked the door with a soft click.

Her expression moved from confusion to mild amusement. "Oh, Mr. Simon," she said, giggling, "I hope you're not serious."

"I am." He dropped the key into his trouser pocket. "Two hundred dollars."

She held Jeremiah's gaze until he looked away. "And here I thought you meant to run me out of town."

"I still may. You watch and see."

She moved beside Jeremiah and slipped her hand into his pocket. His body stiffened; he fought an urge to grab her shoulders and shake her, to crush his mouth against her painted lips. She said, "You're a strange man," and took the key from his pocket.

He yanked her wrist against his chest. The key clattered against the floorboards.

"My goodness." The girl's smile faded into an uneasy grin. "I never dreamed I'd be indebted to such a strange man."

Jeremiah walked to the general store the next morning and purchased a horsehair brush and tin of boot blacking. In the hotel the girl knelt before the window and closed her eyes. He touched her chin to steady himself, then drew the brush across her naked scalp, each line a subtle thrill, as though he were mapping an undiscovered country. When he'd finished, he presented the girl with a hand mirror: she grinned her approval.

That afternoon, Jeremiah stood behind the examiner's chair as the girl wove through the crowded salon. *The knowledge we humbly disseminate is of incalculable value to all men, women, and children,* she proclaimed. *For what knowledge, may I ask, is a tithe as valuable as self-knowledge?* She'd claimed to have studied his texts, but Jeremiah figured she'd read only fifty pages; her explanations began as fact, then strayed into half-truth or pure fancy. He wondered if he should correct her, but the townspeople didn't seem to care. Jeremiah let her flutish voice occupy his mind. Twice he finished examinations to find he had no knowledge of the skull before him, so he created tales flattering enough to please a bitter widow.

That evening in the hotel room Jeremiah locked the door and dumped the day's take onto the bed: fourteen dollars, sixty cents.

She threw her head back and barked in laughter. The lines on her skull had smeared into a black blur. "What's your best day's sum, before today?"

"Eleven dollars."

"My God, it's gorgeous." She grabbed a handful of coins and let them trickle through her fingers. "Listen to that. Sweeter music I never heard."

And that was how it went in Carrier: four days in a crowded salon at the Three Flags Hotel, the girl's voice growing hoarse from shouting above the din. After dinner they walked a circuit of the frigid town, Jeremiah sipping from a flask of brandy while the girl peered into dark shop windows and marveled at the broad, empty streets. Back in the hotel room, he watched her undress in the corner. He felt a frustrating pang of indecision—as though she might scorn him, or remind him that they were strangers—then he moved toward the girl.

When he touched her, she gasped at the coldness of his fingers. Jeremiah held his breath, even as she wrenched his head down to her white throat. He couldn't tell if she was in pain. A low, miraculous thrum rose from her chest, like a cat's purr, and Jeremiah felt a shiver of nervous joy. He ran his lips along her smooth scar. He wanted to move inside the girl, to wear her as a second skin.

Their last night in Carrier, as they lay beneath the sweat-dampened sheet, he touched her wrist and asked about her husband: who he was, and where, and why.

"You're wondering what goat of a man would have me?"

"I'm wondering how he came to be in Detroit, with you in Ohio. It's an unusual arrangement."

She was quiet for a moment, then her voice rose from the darkness: her husband was not a good man. She'd married young, to a cordwainer's apprentice with a clubfoot and jittery laugh, named Ephraim Bennet. He was a layabout and amateur boxer, a no-luck faro player with a temper when he lost. They were happy for a month, then a slow revulsion seemed to grow in him: when he'd finished working her with a hickory switch, he'd shove her outside and lock the cabin door. She'd hidden a straw tick in the shed, and a crock of chilled butter for her welts.

They lived in Yearman, in southern Ohio, until they had nothing to barter and couldn't get credit for a twist of tobacco. Then Ephraim woke her at midnight, loaded their mud wagon, and drove from town with the lanterns shuttered. He sang "Old Rosin the Beau" and hugged the girl like she was his new bride. Three miles outside town he halted the buggy at a crossroad and pissed on the fingerboard pointing toward Yearman.

They'd been in Colson five months when she woke in an empty bed. Ephraim's pistol and Sunday hat were gone; she felt a sudden, startling impulse toward happiness. A week passed, then a month, the girl taking in sewing, which she didn't mind if it meant being free of welts. She sold her husband's Winchester rifle, which he'd left behind, then she sold her pewter. Seven months later she received a grimy letter: *I am in Detroit and Sick as a horse. This Town is hard. Come to 153 Beaubien Street, Mrs. Lasaux's.*

So she went. She took a stage to Aurora, her first time in a Concord wagon, and there was something exciting about being in motion, about entering strange towns at sunset without knowing a soul. She felt wonderfully inconspicuous, like she could do anything she pleased. She'd been traveling two weeks when she saw Jeremiah's handbill outside the Independence Hotel.

"I have to disagree," Jeremiah said, "about solitude being anyway good."

"Queer thing for a man of your profession to say. Is that why you walk around like a dejected coroner? Because you're lonely?"

Jeremiah responded by squeezing her bare shoulder. He said, "Tell me: did you go by stage all the way to New Buffalo? Or did you find rides the way you did with me?"

Her shoulders tensed. "That was a singular occurrence. You looked so handsome in the hotel, with your beautiful hair, and your white gloves. I wondered what kind of man would wear white gloves for that job. I wanted to find out who you were."

She gripped his hand, and for a moment Jeremiah felt thrillingly unmoored, as though he were drifting through an endless sky. Then, like cold fog rolling over him, he understood that his presence was accidental: he was just a man with a buggy headed north. A fool with a dream about a woman who didn't exist, lying beside a girl with an ordinary skull.

Damn all this, he thought. Bless it and damn it. He shut his eyes and pulled the girl closer, and let her hoarse breathing lull him to sleep.

They crossed into Michigan on a rainy Monday, the horizon a pearl-white mist and the road a slurry of mud and dung. Jeremiah uncorked a bottle of Black Aces whiskey, to soften the ride, and they rolled into Keller shouting drunk.

Fronds of frost lay on the windows when they woke. They stayed four days in Keller, then drove north to Grosse Vert, then on to Paulston, the girl singing half-remembered minstrel songs as she drove, while Jeremiah lay on the back bench, chuckling at her invented refrains. A calm pleasure had grown in him, balanced by unease: he found himself watching her, for evidence of her skull's predictions—the strong veneration and wit, the poor adhesiveness and benevolence, the absent ideality. But the girl was as spirited and unpredictable as the weather. Jeremiah wasn't sure if this made him happy or miserable.

Their last night in Paulston, Jeremiah took a room at the Imperial Hotel, and when he opened the door, Sarah collapsed onto the feather bed. "I'll die here," she said, "and heaven won't be nearly as comfortable, I swear." He locked the door and slipped the key into his stocking. It was no more than a gesture, he knew, but the cold key against his ankle had begun to feel routine, and this lent the room a hint of permanence.

She said, "I apologize for stealing your case. I saw you touching those people's heads and taking their money, and I thought, well, anybody can do that. So."

Jeremiah was stunned, silent. Outside, sleet tapped against the windowpane.

"I thought about you afterward. I knew you'd search for me."

"How'd you know that?"

"You were lonely. You looked at each woman like you were starving."

"I was doing research," he said, reddening. "I'm studying women's phrenological characteristics. I'm writing a book."

"You're a kind man." She nodded, her lips pursed. "You treat me very well. Far better than I deserve, I know."

Jeremiah said, "Listen, now," but Sarah shushed him, and pulled him down to the bed.

That night he dreamed. He dreamed of himself and Sarah strolling down Keller's main street, hand in hand. It was summer; Jeremiah wore a black suit that was layered with dust, and Sarah wore a crinoline that remained pure white. They were attending a lecture by Dr. Spurzheim on "Nature's Sexual Laws," and Jeremiah was suffused with joy. It's so simple, he thought, the way a woman's desires can be foretold and understood, and returned. The street ended in a marble pavilion, and a bodiless, booming voice rose from the ground. *Where is the organ of amativeness located?* Jeremiah shouted, *At the base of the skull, the outer portion being animal while the inner is platonic!* The voice asked, *Why do men instinctively adore the female form?* Jeremiah looked at Sarah: her face was grave, as though she were standing at the altar. *In which ways does phrenological analysis of the amorous organs succeed?* the voice thundered. *In which ways does it fail?*

III.

They drove into Detroit on the first day of December, the city beginning as sparse clapboard homes then thickening to brown brick rowhouses and bright storefronts and stone buildings with slender columns. Buggies and omnibuses swarmed the street, filling it with the clop of hooves and creak of wheels and thick, sharp smell of dung. Snow lay in gray streaks on rooftops and shutters and sidewalk edges. Jeremiah drove slowly down Woodward Avenue, as Sarah leaned out the side of the wagon.

"It's so loud," she shouted. "Must be impossible to have decent manners in this city."

"Then you'll feel at home." Jeremiah attempted a chuckle. A tightness had gripped him when they'd glimpsed the city's first gestures, and now his mood was mired in regret. I should have kept west, he thought, pretended I was lost. Or refused to come here at all.

"Stop here," Sarah shouted, and Jeremiah guided the horse to the avenue's margin. He watched her cross the street to a yellow building: the Bank of St. Clair. A clock on the bank's pediment read ten minutes to five.

At five-fifteen she emerged, clutching her capuchin to her chest. "Eagles and slugs, no banknotes." She offered Jeremiah her clenched fists. "Take it. Two hundred dollars."

The coins' weight seemed to fall into the pit of Jeremiah's chest. "You can keep this. You long ago made up your debt."

"I didn't intend any of that to be payment."

"No, goodness, I didn't mean that." He pressed the coins into her hands. "We don't have to stay here. Do you see? We can go by boat down the lake, back to Ohio. To Cleveland, then over to Buffalo." He thought, I could publish a study of her, make us both famous. Make us rich, so we won't have to work, just the two of us alone, in a house with a good field, a porch in front.

"I take sick on boats."

"Then we'll go north, visit the Indians." He grinned stiffly. "You don't have to worry about being scalped. That's some comfort."

"Jeremiah." She squeezed his hands, her mouth set in a pained smile. "There's a hotel beside the bank. Can we stop? I'm so tired."

That night Jeremiah sat on the bank's steps, watching snow slant through a gas lamp's white halo. He'd bought a half-pint of rum, but though the bottle was empty, he wasn't drunk enough: he wanted his thoughts to be effaced, obliterated. He huddled into his greatcoat, feeling the stiff spine of his leather-bound book, then drew it out and turned page after page, until the numbers appeared as tiny smudges. Too many numbers, he thought; a thousand too many. A hundred thousand too many. He knelt, and laid the book and rum bottle in the gutter, then heaped slush over them until he'd formed a mound like a fresh grave. The sight satisfied him but did nothing to raise his spirits.

He walked up Woodward until he finally felt the rum's muddling effects, then asked a passerby directions to Beaubien Street. Jeremiah hurried up Grand River then along Mechanic Street, passing lit-up saloons and dark churches and a huge, shadowy ironworks. The snow had thickened, but Jeremiah was sweating; he unbuttoned his greatcoat and let wind tunnel against his chest.

He stopped outside number 153: a clapboard house with crooked shutters and a railing that was smashed flat, as though it'd been struck by a runaway dray. Jeremiah knocked. A few moments later the door edged open, and a thin, wrinkled woman peered out.

"Mrs. Lasaux?"

"It ain't a decent hour to call."

"I apologize. I'd like to speak with Ephraim Bennet if I could."

The woman squinted at him.

"He arrived a few months ago," Jeremiah offered. "I believe he's a cordwainer."

"He owed me twelve dollars." She opened the door another inch. "Are you kin?"

Jeremiah dug into his pocket, then counted twelve dollars coin into the woman's knobby hand. "I'm his cousin," he said. "Do you have any idea where he went?"

"He's dead," she said. "Died of ague, in his room. Wouldn't have known it, but he smelled dreadful bad."

Jeremiah's heart jumped, then was instantly smothered by shame. I'm glad for another man's death, he thought. God forgive me.

"Had to bang down the door to get him out," she said, opening the door wider. "Cost me ten dollars to mend the lock."

His hand trembled as he offered the woman a banknote. "I'm very sorry for your trouble," he said, backing down the steps. "I hope you'll pray for Ephraim's soul."

"He left some things," she called, but Jeremiah was already crossing the street. He broke into a jog, the frigid air needling his lungs. He ran down Mechanic Street until his chest burned, then staggered to a halt and shouted, a wordless howl. His voice gathered as a frosty cloud then vanished in the black sky.

At the hotel room he stood at the door until his heart settled. Sarah was asleep, her breathing like a slow tide. Her skull lay naked on the pillow, and Jeremiah felt an urge to touch it, and memorize her talents and fears, her desires and instincts and flaws. Instead he knelt beside the bed, watching her eyes dart beneath their lids. He prayed he knew her better than any touch could reveal.

He woke alone the next morning. He'd slept late, a drunken, dreamless sleep, and rose in a cold, bright room that smelled of coffee and fried pork. A soft pang prodded Jeremiah; he dressed and combed his hair, then pushed aside the curtain: snow swirled down Woodward Avenue, painting buggies and street vendors and pedestrians in a scene of merry confusion. On the windowsill Jeremiah's white gloves lay splayed beside Sarah's black.

He grabbed his hat and overcoat and rushed down to the frozen street. He found a grocer and bought a dozen smoked oysters, a wedge of mild cheese, a bottle of champagne and a gleaming red apple, then tucked the bundle inside his coat and hurried back to the hotel. He spread the food on the side table. The room's chamber set had no cup, so Jeremiah sipped the champagne straight from the bottle.

He was finishing the cheese when Sarah opened the door, her capuchin dusted with snow. "You didn't wait long to celebrate," she said. "I'm not even gone, and you've made a banquet."

Jeremiah wiped his mouth on his shirtsleeve. Oyster shells lay scattered at his feet. "Did you see him?"

"I went to Mrs. Lasaux's house on Beaubien Street. I suppose I shouldn't have expected Ephraim to be staying somewhere respectable." She tugged loose her bonnet. "He's very sick. I thought at first it was cholera but his face has a yellowness, like he has the fever. He couldn't get up when I entered his room, he just lay on the bed, moaning. I fed him beef soup. It was the first nourishment he'd had in four days."

Jeremiah heard her as if from a great distance. He couldn't force his lips to form a word.

"He called me *sweetest*. He can be gentle when he's in need—I'd nearly forgotten that." She took her satin gloves from the windowsill and slipped them into her pocket. "Lucky we didn't arrive a week later. I'd never have forgiven myself."

"You don't have to go to him."

"Of course I do."

"You *don't*," Jeremiah said. "I know you don't! Trust me, now—you're just a silly girl."

She seemed to stiffen. Jeremiah tried to meet her eye, but she wouldn't look up from her clasped hands.

"I went to Beaubien Street last night. He's dead, Sarah! I paid his debt, twelve dollars. I talked with Mrs. Lasaux."

A flush bloomed on her cheeks. "You can't keep me. I won't let you." Her voice was thick with stubbornness. "If you keep me, I won't stay. I know it in my heart."

Jeremiah hugged her around the waist, but she twisted against him, her fingernails gouging his wrists. He yanked her hands down and buried his face in her hair, and Sarah shrieked, like a knife scraped against steel. Jeremiah's stomach seemed to fall away. He loosed his grip, and she spun to the room's corner, her eyes shining with fear.

"Forgive me," Jeremiah said. "Please. I'm sorry."

She nodded fiercely, her chest heaving. Then she shoved her bonnet on her head and took up her valise.

On the sidewalk they stood beneath the hotel's awning as snow fell all around them. Jeremiah offered her the skull case. "You can keep these or sell them. I don't care which."

She took the case without looking at him. "I'm nervous, of all things. My goodness, I'm shaking."

Jeremiah said nothing.

"You'll stay here, then?"

He glanced past her, at the blur of carriages, the clamorous rush of people. The city seemed vast and teeming, limitless. "Maybe I'll find some work."

"Then I may see you around town." She kissed him, her lips like cold stones against his cheek, then turned and started down the sidewalk. After a few paces she turned back. "I hope I do see you," she shouted. Then she disappeared in the jostling crowd.

Jeremiah wandered down Woodward Avenue until he reached the riverbank, then sat watching whitecaps flash and chop in the coal-black water. When his knees were stiff with cold, he stepped into a saloon and drank a glass of whiskey, then at a general store purchased a pair of scissors. Back in the hotel room he clipped a long column of hair and watched it fall like a sheaf of wheat into the white basin. When his head was shorn, he lathered his tufted skull and stropped his razor. Gleaming lanes of scalp appeared, his skull's ridges and grooves as familiar as his father's fields. *This is you*, he thought. *This is who you are.*

When he'd finished he stood before the window, in the light, staring at his reflection in the cloudy mirror.

ZILKOWSKI'S THEOREM

HENDERSON slipped into the back of the half-full auditorium and settled into an empty chair, shielding his face with a tattered yellow notepad. Around him, mathematicians stood in groups of three and four, sipping coffee from styrofoam cups and cracking jokes about variational calculus and Zermelo-Fraenkel set theory. Their dreary humor seemed perfectly suited to the auditorium, with its frayed orange carpeting and comfortless chairs and flickering fluorescent lights. *So this is Akron,* thought Henderson. It was neither better nor worse than he'd expected.

The conference was the same every year, the same three hundred people, the same dismal cities: Gdansk one year, then Belfast, now Akron. Where next—Mogadishu, perhaps? Teheran? Henderson recognized and disliked many of the faces he saw; he found these people infinitely more agreeable bound between the covers of journals, their moist handshakes and pungent breath eliminated, their grating voices smoothed by the uninflected diction of mathematics. Henderson ducked his head and scribbled idly on his notepad. He did not want any of his colleagues to notice him, but mostly he did not want to catch the eye of the speaker, Czogloz.

Czogloz was presenting a paper entitled "Perturbation Analysis of Weakly Nonlinear Systems," and as the clock swept past two o'clock he stepped to the podium and flipped on the overhead projector. He looked younger than Henderson had hoped he would: his hairline was anchored firmly to his temples, and his forehead was free of the frown-shaped wrinkles that marked most mathematicians. Four years of assistant professorship had not affected Czogloz much; this seemed unfair to Henderson. Czogloz was sporting a goatee, and wearing a tie made of some shiny purple material that Henderson thought totally inappropriate for a presentation on weakly nonlinear systems. The goatee, Henderson noted, gave Czogloz a demonic air.

"Welcome," Czogloz began, in his lush Hungarian accent, "it's good to see so many familiar faces." Henderson instinctively shrank deeper into his chair, but Czogloz was only following his notes; his gaze never left the podium. He launched smoothly into his presentation, first defining the problem with nitpicky precision, then briefly reviewing related research: Dobujinski's famous 1964 theorem, an obscure series of proofs by a Greek named Kaliardos. Then Czogloz cleared his throat and waded into his own research, his voice rising a half-octave and the words coming faster. Henderson surveyed the dim auditorium: he sensed a grudging respect, a retreat from the skeptical hostility that usually prevailed at the conference. He turned back to the projection screen and began scribbling desperately on his notepad, mentally probing the equations for a tender spot, a place where he could sink a lance.

Czogloz placed a transparency entitled "Summary and Conclusions" on the overhead projector, and as if awakening from a dream the audience shifted slightly. "So it has been shown," Czogloz said, "that stability can be analyzed using classical perturbation analysis, provided the system is weakly nonlinear and locally differentiable." He glanced up from his notes with a reserved but winning smile. "Now. Could I address any—"

"Question," Henderson said. His voice held a nervous, aggressive tone, but he didn't attempt to soften it. He'd been waiting for this moment for so long. "What about the invertibility of the matrix H? You haven't addressed the case where H is singular."

Czogloz peered into the murky reaches of the auditorium. "Could you be more specific, please?"

"Certainly," Henderson said. A few faces in the audience glanced back at him. "On transparency eleven, you claim that if the matrix B is positive definite then H is nonsingular, but you don't discuss the case where B is positive *semi*definite. And of course it's possible that for a dissipative system, B could be positive semidefinite. And thus H could be singular. And thus noninvertible."

Czogloz paused. Slowly, he leafed through his transparencies until he reached number eleven. He placed it carefully on the overhead projector, then turned his back to the audience and stared up at the wide white projection screen. A murmur had surfaced in the auditorium, and there was a tautness in the sound that recalled for Henderson a movie dramatization of a public execution. Czogloz unconsciously stroked his goatee, studying the graceful unfolding of the problem, the ingenious substitution that landed it onto solid footing, then the minor but critical assumption Henderson had attacked.

"Yes, of course." Czogloz cleared his throat. His ears were glowing as if they'd been badly sunburned. "The condition of positive definiteness can be viewed as a restriction of the method. A limitation."

"A limitation? It would seem that your subsequent results are invalidated."

Now the auditorium was silent except for the patient hum of the overhead projector fan. Czogloz nodded stiffly. "That may be correct. I'll have to consider more thoroughly the ... implications."

An appreciative rumble rose from the audience. This type of drama was rare and always welcome: it would be recounted in hushed whispers at the next conference, and the next, and the next after that. Henderson would be viewed with a mixture of fear and respect; his own presentations would become targets for mathematical headhunters. Henderson knew this. He also knew there would be a small crowd awaiting him at the end of the presentation, so before Czogloz could clear his throat forcefully enough to regain the audience's attention, he slipped out the back door.

In his damply air-conditioned Marriott room that evening, as Henderson was packing his garment bag and sipping minibar champagne—a reward for his cruel but delicious victory that afternoon—the telephone rang.

Czogloz's voice held a cheerful lilt. "Hello, John. I hope I haven't disturbed you—you sound quite merry."

Henderson coughed harshly as champagne fizz tickled the back of his throat. He set the plastic tumbler down and wiped his mouth, his palms suddenly damp with perspiration. "Listen, Miklos: there's no point in getting worked up."

"Oh, no, I'm not worked up," Czogloz said. "In fact, I must thank you for pointing out my error this afternoon. In the taxi, going back to the hotel, I realized a solution that avoids the difficulty you pointed out. An extraordinary little solution, actually. It could open an entirely new area of research for me."

"Well. That's wonderful." Henderson stretched the telephone cord into the bathroom and grabbed his shaving kit and toothbrush and stuffed them into the garment bag. "I'm sorry, I can't talk right now, Czogloz. I'm leaving for the airport."

"In an ideal world," Czogloz continued, "you might have been slightly more ... *discreet*. But there it is."

Beneath Czogloz's accent Henderson thought he detected an alcohol-induced slur. The thought of Czogloz drunk made Henderson uneasy, so he quickly zipped his bag and scanned the empty room. "Well, I'm off. I'll see you at the next conference. Or around town, I suppose." Czogloz and Henderson both taught in Boston—Czogloz at a prestigious university in the suburbs and Henderson at a technical college downtown—but Henderson had managed to avoid Czogloz for the past four years.

"I thought we could meet," Czogloz said. "In the hotel bar. Shall we say ... thirty minutes?"

"You're in this hotel?" Henderson glanced nervously at the locked door. "How did you know I was staying here?"

"John, my goodness—you're acting like a character in a horror movie. *Relax*. I'm down the highway, at the Comfort Inn. I'll buy you a drink—Wild Turkey bourbon, if I remember correctly."

"I don't think so, Czogloz. I'd love to catch up on old times, but I'm flying out at eight-thirty."

"There's a matter we should discuss." Czogloz's voice held a dull, melancholy note. It was the voice of a man announcing an unfortunate but inevitable piece of news. "It's Marya, actually."

At the sound of Marya's name a shiver began in Henderson's chest that scurried over every inch of his skin. He felt as though he'd been heated over glowing coals then dunked into an ocean-sized bath of ice water. "What about Marya?"

Czogloz sighed—a deep, troubling soul-sigh. "Too much. Too much for the telephone."

Henderson slumped onto the bed, feeling a familiar ache of yearning and despair, and found himself face to face with his reflection in the armoire mirror. He studied the image dispassionately—the frayed hair, the flabby neck and too-small shirt, the nervous, darting tongue that even to Henderson seemed vaguely obscene—then turned slowly away. "Thirty minutes," he said finally. "I'll need to change my flight."

"Wonderful," Czogloz said. "Do that, John. Change your flight."

Henderson crossed the faded lobby of the Marriott Hotel and paused at the entrance of Chez Georges restaurant. Through the smoky glass doors he saw a row of figures hunched at the bar, and toward the far end he thought he spotted Czogloz's goatee and shiny tie. Henderson rested his hand on the door handle, then backed away and hurried to the men's room and stood in front of an unoccupied urinal and closed his eyes. His heart was fluttering as though he'd just climbed a dozen flights of stairs. Henderson stood at the urinal, exhaling deeply, until he noticed the man next to him frowning; then he flushed and splashed his face in the sink and marched back across the lobby toward Chez Georges, toward Czogloz.

Miklos Zoltán Czogloz, from Budapest via Louisville. They'd met as first-year graduate students at the Michigan Engineering Institute, two aggressive young theorists who disagreed about Marx and Irish beer but agreed that mathematics was a game—the most elaborate, wonderful game, like puzzling out riddles posed by God. That first semester, while ninety inches of snow buried the Institute, Henderson and Czogloz sat across from each other at the pitted oak tables of the Bachman library, working increasingly difficult equations until they could solve them without thinking, like concert pianists playing finger exercises. When the semester ended, they moved into the top half of a decaying Dutch colonial on Mill Street, four blocks from the mathematics building. They smashed a six-dollar bottle of Asti Spumante against the brick windowsill and howled into the frozen December night, and Czogloz christened the house Poincaré Manor, in honor of his favorite mathematician.

And then Henderson met Marya. Marya Zilkowski, from Bialystok, who *liked* mathematics but didn't *love* it, and worried more about whether her kielbasa—which she stuffed by hand, in the bathtub—had too much garlic or black pepper. It was never clear to Henderson why she'd enrolled in graduate school, but he didn't care; no matter why she'd come, he wanted her to stay. Henderson began avoiding the library and instead lay tangled with Marya in his narrow twin bed, listening to Charles Mingus albums or making strenuous love or sampling Polish recipes that Marya had learned from her *babcia*.

She had a California-shaped birthmark, Henderson discovered; she was prone to irrational fits of laughter; she worried that her luxuriant country accent made her sound rude and unintelligent. Marya was flighty—she made important decisions impulsively, as if she were deciding which pair of socks to wear—and although this frustrated Henderson, he envied her ability to change her mind, to implicitly admit she'd been wrong. Marya, in the evening, would cook enormous platters of *kapusta* or *bigos* or *pierogi*, and Czogloz, returning from the mathematics building at midnight or one A.M., would accept a plate of food and sit with Marya and Henderson on the Salvation Army sofa and watch *Hogan's Heroes* reruns. Henderson and Czogloz spoke with unabashed optimism of the control theory problems they would solve—it seemed only a matter of time—while Marya joked about her future restaurant, Mala Warszawa: Little Warsaw, Polish home cooking.

They lived in Poincaré Manor for two years, and during that third summer Henderson flew to Newark for an adaptive control conference. Four days without Marya—he sat at the back of over–air-conditioned conference rooms, his blank notebook before him, and found himself imitating Marya's careless loopy signature. He wrote *Marya Henderson*, and the sight made him fidgety with excitement. He decided to skip Friday's presentations. It was an uncharacteristically impulsive decision. That evening at the airport, hurrying through the drab terminal, he felt a sense of supreme gratitude and wonder, the way he imagined Euler must have felt when he realized $e^{\pi i}+1$ equaled exactly zero, nothing. His sneakers chirped against the tile floor, a sound that inexplicably brought tears to his eyes. At home, as he worked his key in the deadbolt, he thought he heard something odd—a familiar voice with an unfamiliar inflection—but he shrugged it away. His hands trembled against the scratched brass lock.

There was a single terrible moment, when Henderson's garment bag slumped to the floor and Marya glanced up from the kitchen table. She was wearing a blue gingham apron and beneath it was naked. Czogloz was lying on the sitting room floor with a plate of *golabki* beside him and a *Journal of American Mathematics* propped on his chest, and apart from a pair of red sweatsocks he, too, was naked. Henderson stepped back and pulled the door shut. He stood frozen for a moment—he heard Czogloz's plate clatter against the pine floorboards, and Marya cried *czekaj!* in a strangled, unnatural tone—then Henderson was gone, scrambling down the stairs and across the dark quadrangle, toward the mathematics building and the safety of his empty office.

Later there was a telephone call, Marya hiccuping through tears and speaking in anxious half-Polish phrases. *I am stupid, kochana, I am sorry,* she'd said, over and over—but she hadn't offered to take him back. It was a plain, miserable fact: she loved Henderson but she loved Czogloz more. Flighty, flaky Marya had changed her mind. It wasn't something that made sense to Henderson, but then nothing that involved women and love had ever made sense to him. He began sleeping in his office, unable to bear the sight of Marya's bra uncoiled on the floor of Czogloz's room, the smell of her perfume—Chanel No. 5, a classic and melancholy scent—on Czogloz's hand towels in the bathroom. That December, when their lease was up, Henderson at midnight stuffed his clothes and textbooks and yellow notepads into eight liquor boxes and loaded them into a taxi and moved into a studio across the river from the Institute.

And for the next eighteen months, when he saw Czogloz at a seminar or dissertation defense, they talked about ice hockey or control theory and did not mention Marya's name.

But even now Henderson kept the single remaining relic of his and Marya's relationship—a pair of pink cotton panties—in the far reaches of his lower-right desk drawer. Some Friday afternoons, when the Layton building was abandoned and the carillon had tolled its dirge, Henderson found himself closing his office door and leaning back in his armchair, into a slant of sunlight, with the panties crushed up under his chin. Although they'd been washed accidentally, years ago, sometimes Henderson thought he could smell Marya's eastern European tang of garlic and dried leaves, her scent. On the back of the panties, near the tag, was a sight that never failed to twist Henderson's heart: the word MARYA penned in blurry blue ink. He thought he had never seen a name as beautiful or as tragic.

Czogloz, slouched against the bar, did not look as young as he had that afternoon during his presentation. His suitcoat was strewn over a stool and his purple tie was loosened, and he wore the look of a traveler stranded overnight in an airport terminal. As Henderson crossed the room Czogloz rose unsteadily, clutching the bar for support, then shook Henderson's hand with a slightly feminine grip.

"Good to see you, Miklos," Henderson said. "Love your tie."

Czogloz grinned wearily. "Hello, John. It's good to see you, too." There was a sincerity in his voice that Henderson found disarming. "I read your contraction analysis paper in the *JAM*. Wonderful work."

"Not really," Henderson said. "A minor observation surrounded by well-known facts. It didn't deserve publication."

This was the truth and they both knew it, but Czogloz shrugged diffidently. He glanced down at the bar and spread his hands, a conciliatory gesture. "I must tell you, I am not angry about this afternoon. For a while, after the presentation—yes, I was somewhat . . . *perturbed*. But no more."

Czogloz was drinking what looked like cough syrup, and Henderson ordered another and a Wild Turkey for himself. When the drinks arrived, Henderson took a polite sip and said, "So. Marya."

"Marya." Czogloz tilted his glass, watching thick red liquid coat the walls of the tumbler. "We're finally getting married, in October. I don't know if you've heard."

"Hersch told me. Congratulations. I wish you every happiness." Henderson's words were dull and lifeless, a parody of congratulations. "How is she?"

Czogloz frowned into his glass. "She was happy, until a few months ago. She was teaching a Polish cooking course at the BCAE. We put a down payment on a very nice condominium in the city. And then something happened. She 'found religion,' as she likes to say."

"My goodness," Henderson said. "And I have trouble even finding my car keys."

"That's funny," Czogloz said, without smiling. "I'd almost forgotten about your interesting sense of humor." Czogloz signaled for another drink and tapped the base of his tumbler against the bar until it arrived. "And now she is carrying things too far—even the priest agrees. She called Krakow last month to tell her mother about the time she stole six hundred thousand *złoty* from her grandmother's purse. The poor woman! Seventy years old, listening to her only daughter tell her she's a thief."

"A conversion," Henderson mused. "Jesus. Who'd have guessed?" The bourbon was warming him into loquaciousness, and the strangeness of the story warmed him further. He was glad, he reflected, that he'd changed his flight and come tonight. He was glad Czogloz had called. "I suppose it's nice for her, but how many people is she hurting? Her mother, you. Who else?"

Czogloz nodded. "I was hoping you could help."

"And why would I do that?"

"For Marya. And for me. It is making things . . . difficult."

Henderson stirred his drink with his pinkie, then licked his finger. "Really? How difficult?"

Czogloz nodded, as if he'd been expecting the question. "She will no longer go to horror movies, which is something we both—we all—loved. She spends weeknights at Bible study or adoration, then berates me for not attending with her. She's begun listening to Christian folk music."

"That's it? Movies and shitty music?"

"She told me last week she was reconsidering the wedding."

Henderson paused with the bourbon nearly to his lips, then recovered and took a long, casual sip. He was not completely surprised; it was just like Marya to dither over something so important. Czogloz's lips were pursed; he was staring at the tall, ornate peppermill that stood in an alcove behind the bar like a religious icon. "Do you know, John, that Catholics believe Jesus Christ rose from the dead?" Czogloz grinned bemusedly. "That he hopped up, stone dead, and strolled away?"

Henderson could not imagine Marya kneeling in a church,

or praying, or lifting a gaudy gold chalice to her lips; she was so thoroughly *carnal*. When he thought of Marya, he most often thought of cooking—the tightly rolled *golabki*, the swollen, bursting kielbasa, the thick Bulgarian wine—or he thought of sex.

Henderson had never been drawn to religion; the notion of God seemed as abstract to him as nonlinear control theory did to most other people. Some late nights, the sheets in knots and his forehead filmed with sweat, Henderson found himself yearning for some nebulous *goodness* into which he could cast his irritation and anxiety and self-doubt. In his half-dreaming state he envisioned the faux-antique wishing well that stood in the lobby of the nearby McDonald's. When he woke the next morning, however, he felt a caustic mixture of skepticism and shame. For what was there to believe in? The ability of people to grow accustomed to even the cruelest discomfort. The dusky accumulation of regret with every passing year. The flow of electrons from low potentials to higher ones. Beyond that—what?

"There's more," Czogloz said. "There's the matter of her Ph.D."

The restaurant's jazzy music seemed to pause, and the other patrons' voices fell mute, as though they were speaking through cotton. Henderson watched Czogloz study the empty bottom of his glass. "She wants to give up her Ph.D. And she wants to announce the truth, in the *JAM*."

Henderson clutched Czogloz's wrist. "Jesus, Miklos. Stop her."

"She's very serious about it," Czogloz said, extracting his wrist with a gentle but firm tug. "She says the situation has always made her feel terrible."

Henderson slumped against the bar and mechanically signaled for another round. He felt a numbness that went far beyond the effects of the bourbon. He felt like a dental patient dulled by Novocain, indifferently watching the world move before him.

"You know," Czogloz said, "I think it's the best work you've ever done. Zilkowski's theorem—I *knew* it wasn't actually hers. She didn't care about it, it was nothing to her. And yet . . ." He trailed off. "Such beauty. A beautiful proof."

Henderson shrugged bleakly. "I was inspired, I suppose."

"It must have pained you to see it published under someone else's name."

"Not at all," he said, with more feeling than he'd intended. "I was happy for Marya. I wanted her to be happy."

"Happiness." Czogloz grinned ruefully. "A difficult condition to achieve."

It had started five months after Henderson moved out of Poincaré Manor: she'd called one chilly May morning, while Henderson was struggling against an impulse to draw the blinds and stay in bed until noon. Marya's voice sent a warm shiver down through his thighs. "Are you well?" she'd asked, and it was all he could do not to laugh bitterly. "Perfect," he'd said. "How are you?"

She told him about her mother's arthritis, about the hot, needling pains in her own wrists, about the pumpkin-colored sweater she'd knitted for her sister's son, Stefan. Her voice slipped into a languorous sigh, and suddenly it was as if she'd never done the thing she'd done: they talked about Reagan, and Charlie Parker. They talked about sex. She told him details about herself and Czogloz that Henderson could not bear to hear but that thrilled him nonetheless. But there was a problem, she admitted. Her dissertation—she was stuck. The feeling, she explained, was like trying to run a marathon without understanding how even to crawl. "Who knows? Maybe I'll return home," she said. "Maybe it's time to open Mala Warszawa."

"Don't," Henderson said. "Please don't. Give me six weeks—a month."

Henderson went to the library. Marya was studying a class of problems not too distant from his own research, and within a week he'd discovered some curious connections. That next Sunday there was a feverish stretch of hours when equations seemed to fall all around him, like ripe fruit from a tree. He scribbled them down as fast as he could write. Monday morning, exhausted, he called Marya's apartment to tell her the news, but Czogloz answered the phone. Henderson closed his eyes and hung up.

It happened occasionally: the Ph.D. student who flared like a brilliant comet then disappeared. Marya's dissertation committee, after her defense, convened for only seven minutes—*seven minutes*—then burst from the conference room to tell her she'd passed, that she was now Dr. Marya Zilkowski. And she had not published a single paper since.

"So," Czogloz said, setting his empty glass on the bar, "the final reason I called you tonight: Marya and I would like to invite you to dinner next week, at our condominium."

The thought of sitting down to dinner between Czogloz and Marya seemed so ludicrous to Henderson that he stared at Czogloz for a long moment without saying anything. "Dinner," he said finally.

"Marya's been experimenting with new recipes—Polish-

French, Polish-Cantonese." Czogloz shrugged. "Fusion cuisine, I suppose."

Henderson rose unsteadily from the stool. He felt flustered and weary. And drunk. "No French," he said. "No Cantonese—just Polish. Tell her I'll come only if she cooks plain Polish."

Czogloz nodded. "I'll ask her to make *bigos*." He looked up at Henderson with a clear-eyed expression that, for a moment, seemed almost wistful. "It was your favorite, I believe. Yes?"

"They were all my favorites," Henderson said.

The next night, back in Boston, Henderson reclined on his battered sofa and allowed his mind to explore the horrible and fascinating possibility of being exposed as the author of Zilkowski's theorem. There would be a minor scandal; conversation in the coffee room at the next conference would fall to a hush when he entered. In a perverse way, Henderson realized, it would enhance his reputation. But tenure review committees were not known for their wit or compassion.

Yet what would it matter? At worst, his tenure review would be scathing; he would be asked to find another job. Truth was, Henderson disliked academia. He disliked the bitchy tediousness of faculty meetings; he disliked the endless discussions with self-absorbed undergraduates, who were uncertain if they should major in mathematics or Spanish literature. Often Henderson found himself nostalgic for his days as a graduate student, days where he'd spend eleven hours huddled in a study carrel, stopping only to microwave a frozen burrito or watch snow drift past the Bachman library windows. It had been a lonely but painless existence.

The Russian theorists would understand, Henderson thought idly. They would understand the concept of theorems written for the sake of romance. The Russians had an appreciation for the noble, doomed gesture, but others—the Germans, the Japanese, the Americans—who could say? Henderson willed his mind into a state of blankness. Outside his apartment window, a man spoke half of a conversation into a cellular phone. *Can't do eight hundred*, the man said. *Nine fifty, absolute lowest. Break my balls lowest.* His life was simple, thought Henderson. He knew nothing of Zilkowski's theorem.

He shuffled to the kitchen and poured a pint of milk into a saucepan, but the smell of it warming made his stomach curdle, and he dumped it down the sink. He knelt, and from the far reaches of the cabinet retrieved a bottle of Wild Turkey. A gauzy film of dust lay over the bottle and made it seem ancient, an artifact from a less enlightened time. Henderson poured a tall finger of bourbon into a coffee mug and shuffled to the sitting room. He rifled through his cassettes and picked out one of Feynman's lectures, then flopped onto the sofa. The voice of the genius physicist filled the small apartment, but instead of soothing Henderson, as it usually did, it only made him feel suddenly and painfully aware of his own mediocrity. And yet Henderson didn't stop the cassette. Instead he got to his feet and turned the volume up—way up, blasting, loud enough for all the neighbors to hear.

Czogloz and Marya's condominium was on Commonwealth Avenue near Kenmore Square, and as Henderson peeled off the I-93 exit ramp, he locked the doors, as he always did when he drove into the city. On the porch, listening to the muted chime of the doorbell, he found himself unhappily reviewing his recent conversation with Czogloz. He'd been taken advantage of again: enlisted to help pacify the woman who'd dumped him, by the man she'd dumped him for. That woman! Not only had she lured him into writing her dissertation, now she was punishing him for doing it. A bitter taste rose in Henderson's mouth, and he spat into the cluster of violet tulips alongside the porch. And people like Czogloz get National Science Foundation grants, he thought, while Henderson has to beg for research funding. He had subconsciously slipped into the third person, as he did during moments of severe anxiety.

The door opened, and there was Czogloz: wearing faded jeans and a yellow polo shirt, looking decidedly more relaxed than he had in Akron. Behind him stood Marya. She had shrunk slightly, it seemed to Henderson, and her hair had darkened from iced-tea brown to near-black, but otherwise she was the same woman he remembered with such painful specificity. She was wearing an orange blouse and a short black skirt, with sheer purple tights—an oddly sexy, Marya-like combination—and the sight of her, standing before him, caused in Henderson a warm, liquid rush of desire. She wiped her hands on a dishtowel and beamed at Henderson as he stepped inside.

"The brilliant scholar arrives! It's great to see you, John." She took him by the shoulders and kissed him, right cheek then left, a one-two combination that left Henderson dizzy. "Come in, please—everything's ready."

Czogloz led Henderson through a quick tour of the condo—unremarkable, save for a dim, musky bedroom strewn with tangled heaps of clothes, which Czogloz hurried past—then ushered him into an airy dining room with polished oak floorboards and a bay window. The room bore unmistakable traces of Czogloz and Marya—a framed mathematical journal offprint, a stereo cluttered with worn, sleeveless records—and the sight of such objects in close proximity piqued Henderson's displeasure. It was a warm evening, and the windows were thrown open; faint nasal rhythms of a Red Sox broadcast drifted in from a neighbor's television. Czogloz offered Henderson a glass of murky red wine, and Henderson downed it in three swallows. "You must be mortgaged to the hilt," he said to Czogloz. "Not bad for an assistant professor."

"The basement floods," Czogloz said, "and the radiators are temperamental. Other than that . . . we're happy."

Marya appeared from the kitchen with a tray of *golabki*. *Golabki*—a rush of intense sensation filled Henderson's chest, so suddenly that he thought he might sob. The memory of a particular August night came to him: *golabki* and the same thick red wine; he and Marya dining cross-legged on the floor, in the languorous heat, in their underwear; a scratchy Monk record blasting from the bedroom. That woman! He took a seat at the table and speared one of the dumplings with his fork and bit it in half.

"I hope it's not too spicy," Marya said. "I remember you liked spicy."

Henderson turned to her. "So. Czogloz—Miklos—told me about your conversion. I would say I'm happy for you, but that wouldn't be completely accurate."

Marya looked at Henderson with tender curiosity, like a child examining a small, injured animal. "Same old John. You never did like small talk, did you?" She sipped her wine and grinned. "I know, you think it's just one of my silly ideas. It's not. Truly."

"I suppose you want my approval for your 'announcement' in the *JAM*? I suppose that's the purpose of this dinner?"

Now Marya laughed, and shot Henderson a wry glance. "John, please—I would like your approval, yes. I won't deny that."

"My approval," Henderson said. "Let me see: you publish a retraction, walk away with a clear conscience, and I get—what? Mocked by the tenure committee. Shunned at conferences."

"You get my gratitude," Marya said, covering his hand with hers. "You get the knowledge that you've made me happy. That's all I can offer, John. What else do I have?"

"For God's sake," Henderson said, suddenly—infuriatingly—thrilled by Marya's touch. "Do you really think this is necessary? Think of all the fools with Ph.D.'s, and you, an intelligent person who deserves one! It's a victimless crime."

"No crime is victimless," Marya said, with a shrug. "When you find religion, you begin to understand that."

Henderson shook his head in disgust: Marya had changed. She seemed duller, less spontaneous. And her accent, which had once sounded so alluringly foreign, had flattened into a quasi-American drawl. Beside Marya, Czogloz was staring out the bay window with a vacant, terminal expression on his face. Outside, the Red Sox broadcast had increased in volume, the surflike roar of the crowd washing over the commentators' chatter; it was tied at three in the fifth inning.

They finished the *golabki* in silence. Czogloz cleared their plates and emerged from the kitchen with bowls of steaming *bigos,* and when he departed to fetch another bottle of wine, Henderson rested his elbows on the table and stared at Marya. "So now you want to be forgiven," he said. "I thought you people had priests for that."

Marya shot him a quick, tight-lipped glance. "It's a matter of conscience," she said quietly. "I did awful things, John. Cheating on you. Plagiarizing. Calling you in the morning when Miklos was gone. It wasn't right."

"It was nothing. Nothing happened! We talked about control theory, which—last time I checked—is not a sin."

"It was wrong. I was wrong to treat you the way I did." She nodded matter-of-factly, as Czogloz returned with the wine. "For several years I was very unhappy."

"And now you are happy," Henderson said.

Marya looked up at him, the expression on her face gliding from suspicion to resentment to tenderness, all within a half-second. "Yes," Marya said. "I'm happy."

Henderson started to speak, then shook his head and swallowed a long gulp of wine. He wanted Marya to be happy, but not this way; sneaking into happiness through the back door of religion was too easy, a fool's bargain. He felt a surge of angry restlessness. He downed the rest of the wine and wiped his mouth with the back of his hand.

"Okay, fine. I'll make you a deal." Henderson motioned toward the open window and the chatter of the baseball broadcast. "If the Red Sox win, you have my blessing. Publish your retraction. Ruin my career. Be happy. But if the Sox lose— sorry, Marya. I guess you'll just have to live with your conscience. Like the rest of us."

"John! What are you—what do you mean?" Marya asked. She and Czogloz were staring at him with horrified expressions on their faces. "Please, John, do this for me. For our friendship."

"Henderson," Czogloz hissed, "this is too important to trivialize. For all of us."

But Henderson leaned back in his chair and shrugged. For so long he'd played by the rules, and lost; now he was willing to give fate a chance.

Czogloz stared at the television in the corner as if it were a bizarre contraption he'd never seen before, then slowly flipped through the channels until he found the game. They moved their chairs around the table and watched in silence: the Red Sox scored in the sixth and eighth, but the Tigers tied it with a three-run homer in the top of the ninth. The game went into extra innings. Marya sat forward in her chair, hugging herself in concentration, but Henderson found himself unable to focus his attention. He felt as vacant and detached as the Hood Dairy Company blimp on the screen, drifting high above the ballpark. He drank a third glass of wine and then a fourth, watching dusk deepen through the bay window, the streaky pink and orange of the horizon recalling for him a freakish aurora borealis he'd once seen at the Institute. At one point he became aware of Czogloz studying him, but when he glanced over, Czogloz turned away.

The Tigers eked out a run in the top of the eleventh—a single, a wild pitch, two long fly balls—and in the bottom of the inning the first two Red Sox grounded to the shortstop. A desperate rumble rose from the crowd. "What now?" Henderson said, to the side of Marya's face. "What happens now? You go ahead with more confessions, you make yourself feel better, then what? What about the people around you? Forgiveness doesn't come so easily, Marya." She didn't look at him. "Religion has as many unanswered questions as mathematics," Henderson insisted. "Wait and see."

Just then the volume leaped to a roar, and the camera panned sharply upward; Henderson spotted the ball arcing high above the stadium, a brilliant streak against the grainy sky. The ball seemed to hang motionless for an instant; then as if swatted by an invisible hand it began to plummet. Marya clapped her hands together in astonishment. The Detroit right fielder sprinted back to the warning track and then to the wall, and as the ball cleared the fence, he leaped, his glove reaching back into the bullpen, then stumbled away from the fence with his glove held high. He'd caught the ball; a moan escaped from the Boston crowd. The Detroit right fielder pumped his fist and flipped the ball from his glove to his bare hand. He trotted slowly toward the dugout.

Czogloz released a hiss of breath. "I closed my eyes. I've always hated that aspect of sports, the tension." He seemed to want to say more but stayed quiet. On the screen, players were shaking hands with one another and shuffling toward the dugouts.

Henderson sat with his arms crossed over his chest. He turned to Marya, who seemed to be staring at something just beyond the television set. Her lips were drawn into a thin, determined line, and her hands were clasped, as if she were praying. "If I were a cruel man," Henderson said, "I'd point out a moral here."

"But you're not cruel. You're generous and intelligent, and kind." Marya took Henderson's hand. "You're not cruel, John. Are you?"

The next morning Henderson reclined in his stained leather chair, stirring a mug of coffee with the gnawed end of a ballpoint pen. It was not yet seven o'clock, and the Walter H. Layton mathematics building was quiet. Henderson had never been in his office quite so early, and was surprised at how much he enjoyed the deep, luxurious silence; soon the first graduate students would arrive, unshaven and reeking of last night's stirfry, then the undergraduates with eight A.M. lectures, then the staff assistants and UPS men, and the building would begin to exude its normal levels of tension and haste. Henderson sipped his coffee and studied the dusty vectors of sunlight arrayed across his desk. It occurred to him that he would miss his office, if he were asked to leave. It was the only place at the university he felt truly at ease.

The mailbox icon on his Unix desktop was blinking: one new message, from Czogloz, time-stamped 2:17 A.M.

Dear John, it began, and Henderson paused, momentarily taken aback at the sight of such a personal greeting. *I am writing to thank you. You have made Marya very happy, and therefore you have made me very happy. A great weight has been lifted from her: she sits now at the table composing a menu for our wedding, which will be in May, and the smile on her face is truly wondrous. I have no words to describe it. You will be invited to the wedding, of course, and I hope you will attend.*

The editor of the JAM *has agreed to publish a brief note in the December issue regarding the "misunderstanding," as he terms it. I regret this. I regret also that Marya has drafted a letter to the regents of the Institute asking that they revoke her Ph.D. I was unable, finally, to discourage her.*

I must tell you that Marya believes you possess great kindness. I told her this is not true—I hope you understand. Because it is not true, is it? You are not kind. Marya claimed that your recent generosity was proof of the spirit working within you. I did not have a response to that statement. It seemed—dare I say?—plausible.

I am too tired to write more, but must thank you again for what you've done. I do not completely understand why you've done it, but am grateful nonetheless. Thank you.

Your friend,

Miklos

Henderson reread the message, then clicked "delete." He logged off the computer. He leaned back in his chair, feeling vaguely certain that he should feel good about what he'd done—or what he'd allowed to happen—yet he did not feel good. For who, in the end, would benefit? Marya. Czogloz, by extension. And Henderson—as usual—would be left worse off, lower down, unhappier. Was it possible to find happiness in its pure state, unalloyed by sorrow? Sometimes it seemed so, but often Henderson was convinced it was impossible. Happiness was a zero-sum game: for one to become happy, another must find despair. For so long Henderson had been on the wrong side of the equation.

With this thought in his mind Henderson took a small padded envelope from his desk drawer and printed Czogloz's university address on it, then stuffed Marya's pink panties inside and stapled the envelope shut.

Outside, the sun had risen above the computer science building and a breeze was stirring the newly fallen leaves. Four students in identical blue T-shirts and khaki shorts were strolling down West Street, untroubled by the early autumn chill and all it implied: syllabuses, homework, exams. New junior faculty, new emeriti. Tenure reviews. Arrivals and departures. Henderson watched them for a moment, envious of their cheery indifference, then hurried north, toward the faculty parking lot.

Driving across town, he switched on the radio but didn't bother tuning any particular station. He parked near the mathematics building of Czogloz's college and inside found an inter-campus mailbox. He hesitated for a moment—the envelope resting on the lip of the mail slot, the panties' weight almost imperceptibly slight—then dropped the package in and double-checked to make sure it had reached bottom. No return address, no postmark, the monotonous blocky printing; Czogloz might suspect who'd sent it, but he'd never know for sure. *Fine,* thought Henderson. *Let him wonder.*

He hurried back to his car and drove past the edge of campus, past the Portuguese neighborhood, to where the houses possessed a faded shabbiness. On a whim he turned down a leaf-strewn, deserted side street. He felt a dark tugging, of something like remorse, but he pushed it away. He parked the car and began to walk, past a Laundromat, then a bank, then a fish market. Across the street was a church, a steepled stone building with broad concrete steps and a bright stained-glass window above the doors. A homeless man in an army fatigue jacket was sitting on the steps, smoking a cigarette. A sign near the sidewalk read: JESUS SAVES SAT 6 SUN 9 1030 1215.

Henderson crossed the street and climbed the steps and pulled open the tall, heavy wooden doors. Inside, sunlight filtered through rows of high windows and settled over the empty pews. The air smelled of incense and old, moist stones. He took a seat in the rearmost pew and stared straight up at the graceful geometry of the vaulted ceiling. It was a gorgeous place, he had to admit: the emptiness, the silence, the warm, dense air like a blanket draped over his shoulders. Somewhere outside a car alarm squealed, the sound muffled and hollow in the cavernous church.

He recalled a story he'd once heard, about Euler's "proof" of God's existence to Diderot: $\frac{a+b^n}{n} = x$, so God must exist. Ridiculous, of course. But then there was Pascal's argument: that reasonable men should believe in God, because the potential payoff of heaven far outweighed the risk of hell. Henderson sat with his hands clasped, biting his lower lip. If

Pascal had known probability theory, he thought, he could have formalized his argument. It was a shame.

A young priest walked down the aisle carrying a pair of ivory candles, and Henderson found himself trying to catch his eye. The thought occurred to him that he, John Henderson, could join the priesthood. His body quivered at the thought, a sharp rush of fear and excitement. They took anyone who applied—wasn't there some rule? *Look at me,* Henderson thought, his gaze fixed on the priest's downcast face. He could join the priesthood and spend entire afternoons thinking about faith, about forgiveness. Yes. He could stand before a congregation, and tell them what it meant to be lonely and full of fear. *Look at me,* he thought. *Please. Look at me.*

But the priest hurried past, his cassock rustling softly.

THE CONFESSIONAL APPROACH

I AM sitting in the back of a SMART bus, on my way to Royal Oak, sweating. In my purse is a newspaper—to hide behind, as in bad movies—and three large navel oranges to sustain me through my stakeout. I'm not sure why I'm following Freddy, but lately I've been dreaming of lathes: shiny yellow Nova X3000s with adjustable headstocks. In the dreams I'm leaning naked over an X3000 in the middle of a huge meadow, and mannequins that seem to be made of maple or maybe birch are scattered nearby, standing at attention like overgrown clothespins. It's a strangely menacing dream—I fear that the mannequins will bonk me with their clublike arms (which sounds silly but is in fact terrifying)—and when I wake, I feel a buzz of panic and relief surrounded, inexplicably, by traces of nostalgia.

Freddy kissed my cheek this morning at 8:45—stubble, Ivory soap, stale incense—and I caught the 9:03 from Woodward Avenue to downtown Royal Oak. Now the bus heaves to a stop at the corner of Eleven Mile Road and Troy, leaving me standing on the sidewalk feeling distinctly guilty but also strangely exhilarated. It feels good to be outside in the sun instead of bent over a lathe in my dim workshop. I know Freddy is working the small downtown area, and as I hurry toward William Street, I see him: stepping out of a hip secondhand store called Rebop, hauling the dummy case with both hands. I settle onto a sidewalk bench, unfold the newspaper, and peer overtop the business section. Freddy, obviously sweating in his clingy pin-striped suit, lugs the heavy black case down the crowded sidewalk. He does not look like a man with a guilt-wracked conscience. He does not look particularly happy or graceful, as he pauses in front of Noir Leather, a fetish-wear shop, mops his brow with the sleeve of his suitcoat, then trundles the dummy case into the store.

Freddy's not entirely comfortable as a salesman. He tries to look businesslike—his suit is endearingly earnest, almost Mormon in its single-breasted seriousness—but his tie-dyed tie gives him away. And then there's his hair: he does his best to gather it into a ponytail, but invariably small strands escape and vault skyward, giving him a frazzled, angelic air.

In an attempt to make his job feel less predatory, Freddy's developed a sales philosophy based on what he calls "the confessional approach." During his pitch he shares something personal with the potential buyer—he confesses a weakness or fear, or affirms a mutual dislike. Freddy's theory is that this builds intimacy and trust, and leads to increased sales for our company and a clearer conscience for himself. So far his theory—the part about increased sales—is unproved.

I have the newspaper spread across my knees and am peeling a navel orange when I notice Freddy across the street, his hand raised to block the sun, squinting at me. A warm plume of guilt rises to my cheeks; I look quickly away. When he's halfway across the street I glance up, feign a surprised expression, and wave.

"Hey!" I shout. "What are you doing here?"

Freddy clambers up the curb, the dummy case knocking against his knee. "I *thought* that was you. Weird—from across the street you looked sort of like my mother. I mean, your hair, the way it's sort of flippy today, or maybe those sunglasses..." He shakes his head to clear the image. "Wow. For a second it was fairly disturbing."

"I needed some tools from Farritor's—a new veiner," I explain. "It was sort of an emergency."

He nods, tapping his foot on the pavement, a sound that sets me on edge. Have I disrupted something? Freddy's been acting strange lately, overly moody and pensive, very un-Freddylike. On Tuesday he hastily ended a telephone call when I wandered into the office, and when I asked about the call he said, "Nothing! Nothing—a new client, hopefully." My thoughts flashed back to the incident last March, triggering pangs of doubt and regret. On Wednesday Freddy brought home a magnificent bouquet of purple tulips. This sent tiny sparks shooting through me, which I later realized were warning flares. When I asked about the tulips, he shrugged. "They looked sort of lonely. I don't know. They made me happy." He kissed my forehead. "You make me happy."

Now he slumps beside me on the bench and tugs at his tie. "You know what the woman in Noir Leather just told me? *We prefer mannequins that look like people.*" He wipes a glaze of sweat from his upper lip, and I notice that his cheeks and forehead are dotted with pale pink blotches, the prelude to a full-blown nervous rash. "She was wearing a latex leotard. Can you imagine, on a day like today? It distracted me, I think. It threw me off my pitch."

"How about this: I'll buy you lunch," I suggest. "Anything you want. We'll go to that Ethiopian place I hate."

"Actually, there's a meeting—it's sort of semi-important. It's good that you're here, Judith. It's fate, even though you think that's stupid." Freddy takes a red bandanna from his pocket, blots his forehead, and stands up. He checks his watch. Then he does something troubling: he takes the bandanna back out of his pocket and blots his forehead again.

"Hey, whoa," I say, pulling him down to the bench and loosening his tie. "Take a breath. You look a little wobbly, Fred."

"Yes, I don't feel great," he says. "In fact, I've been feeling extremely shitty this past week. Maybe you've noticed."

I nod cautiously. (The incident from last March replays in my head: Freddy frozen on the sofa, shirtless, watching Oprah interview a small, wrinkled man; the ribbons of diffuse sunlight on our apartment wall; the sweet smell of marijuana.)

"Listen: I could use a drink." He checks his watch again and sighs. "Can I buy you a drink? We'll have a drink, and talk. About lunch."

Freddy tells me about the guns in a juice bar. We're sitting at the front window watching children in the park across the street play a brutal game of dodgeball. Their shouts echo faintly in the air-conditioned shop. Freddy sips his carrot smoothie and tells me about the woman, Kennison, and her plan, which is to dress my mannequins in camouflage, place them in various locations around her thirty-acre shooting club, and let higher-paying members of the club shoot them with rifles. Apparently Kennison explained this over the phone on Tuesday. "She was *proud* of the idea," Freddy says, a hint of confusion in his voice. "She said her daughter came up with it."

"This was a girl's idea?"

Freddy nods. "A fourteen-year-old."

The prospect of someone blowing the head off one of my dummies is momentarily stunning. "So—what?—this is what you wanted to talk about? The mannequins?"

"It's been bothering me." Freddy stares at the children across the street. "I've been feeling extremely terrible this week. I had this feeling—"

"You were acting funny, I noticed."

"—like there was something following me. Like when you're walking up Jefferson at night, past the sleazy motels? I felt like that. I felt like I was being followed by this huge, invisible . . . something." He sips his smoothie pensively.

"You felt guilty, you mean."

"I guess so. So what? So I felt guilty."

Guilt is a common theme in our relationship. Freddy feels guilty for the incident last March, for eating green grapes and iceberg lettuce, for participating in capitalism, for not suffering enough, for not loving me enough. I feel guilty for quickening my pace as I walk past homeless men in Hart Plaza; beyond that, not much. I used to feel guilty for not feeling guilty about what Freddy feels guilty about. (I hid this from him, guiltily.) But I kicked that complicated habit; instead I started smoking.

"You're allowed to be upset about this," Freddy says now. "I mean, they're your dummies. Your *art*. And you're allowed to be upset at me for having anything to do with this woman.

Jesus! What kind of woman owns a gun range? This is the same kind of weirdo who used to be at those Reagan rallies in Ann Arbor."

"This isn't a big deal," I say. "This is called *overreacting*, Freddy. You're overreacting."

Freddy looks at me with shocked incomprehension. "Yes! Judith, this is a big deal. This is most definitely a big deal. I mean, I've been extremely full of self-loathing this week, feeling terrible, not telling you. Which is stupid because I have no secrets from you."

"So why didn't you tell her to forget it?" I say, trying to hide my annoyance.

"I just didn't. We were talking on the phone. She mentioned that she owned a gun range. She said it—*I'm looking for some mannequins for my gun range*. Then she started talking about something else, and I didn't say anything." He shrugs. "I just didn't."

Freddy has turned down contracts before. Eleven months ago we got a call from a sporting goods company in Grand Rapids who wanted to use our mannequins to advertise fishing apparel. Freddy, his voice *profundo* so I could hear him in the shop, told the woman he'd rather swim laps across the Detroit River than sell them our dummies. Apparently the company was involved in a high-profile lawsuit over its allegedly bigoted hiring practices. The lawsuit was later dropped.

"Maybe we should just skip the meeting," he suggests now. "Blow it off—go see a movie or something. We don't need this woman."

"Actually, we do need her. Hello? I have nothing on the lathe right now, Freddy. Nothing."

He nods. "I'm completely aware of that."

"Listen—how many times have I heard you preach about open-mindedness, and being a good listener? Maybe you misunderstood her, Fred. Maybe it's not as bad as it sounds."

"I doubt that. Anyway, I said I'd meet her at twelve at Mykonos. Can you believe that? I somehow offered to buy her lunch." He shakes his head in disbelief. "I'm buying lunch for Republicans. This is the kind of person I've become."

"Let's hear what she has to say," I say. "Maybe you were right—maybe this is fate."

"I made a big mistake. I feel sort of sick." Freddy gives me a curdled-milk look, checks his watch, and stands up. "All right, I guess. How's my collar?"

I straighten it. "Perfect." I smooth his wiry hair against his head and hold my hand to his damp cheek. "You look very businesslike."

"Businesslike," he says ruefully. "Wonderful."

Before he sold dummies, Freddy was a psychology major and big-shot student activist. We first met on a drizzly October Monday on the steps of the Michigan Student Union, at a UAW rally. I'd gone with my friend Tania to see a real protest—two awestruck eighteen-year-old physics majors, stoned on a joint given to us by our dormitory student adviser. We had no idea what we were shouting about. Our morality was abstract; it was like integral calculus. In high school I'd been a nerd, the girl who wore too-short corduroys and smelled of pine shavings, and that afternoon I realized that I loved rallies, I loved being stoned, I loved the idea of fighting something, and losing but being *right*. Freddy's hair was longer than mine, and when he marched it swung like a ropy pendulum.

He shouted himself hoarse and came down with a flu, which I treated in my dormitory bed with hot tea and vigorous intercourse. (My mistake, Tania later claimed, was the hot tea; in serving tea I unwittingly played into a classic Florence Nightingale fantasy; Freddy's image of me was forever trivialized; all men are pigs.) I moved into his apartment three weeks later, Freddy still nursing his flu, which he blamed on the university administration. When he received a bill for antibiotics, he sent it to the university president along with a bitchy letter demanding payment in full.

Freddy's apartment was in the attic of a Victorian house on Fuller, with peeling yellow wallpaper and a coffin-sized bathroom, and we lived there for four years in a rarefied state of happiness: absolute, idiotic bliss attainable only by undergraduates. On the night of my graduation, Freddy led me up the rickety attic stairs to the roof. We sat at the edge with our feet dangling in space, watching the Huron River fade into grainy dusk then into darkness. Freddy had been serving cappuccino at the Espresso Royale Café since his own graduation, but now he had a plan: handmade mannequins, hardwood limbs, articulated joints. Our own shop, our own hours. Our own agenda.

I'd been carving wood since I was a high school nerd in tooshort corduroys. I told Freddy I loved him. I told him I'd never really cared about physics. I told him his plan sounded perfect.

Two years ago, our first year in business, we posted a loss of two thousand eight hundred dollars. In June we sold my beloved '84 Chevette to pay the electricity bill. We moved out of our airy attic on Fuller and into a one-bedroom above a Middle Eastern restaurant, on the east side of Detroit. We tried to pretend it wasn't so bad; I hung new curtains and sprinkled boric acid like holy water to ward off roaches, Freddy painted our bedroom purple and swirled orange. But it was hopeless. Our second week we came home to find the ceiling leaking brown, silty water into our mattress. In the evening we ate across from each other in silence. It seemed impossible that we'd been so quickly reduced to this: eating canned kidney beans and rice. At night, before I fell asleep, a feeling suspiciously like desperation—constricted breathing, sweats, teary anxiety—crept over me. What happened, I wanted to know, to people who failed in a city like Detroit?

Freddy stayed optimistic. "We're building our client list," he explained calmly, one discouraging Sunday night. "We have enough money to get by, we have our apartment—which, okay, is somewhat shitty, but not completely terrible—our car, food on the table. What more do we really, honestly need?"

I had a list taped to the refrigerator of things we needed: an unstained mattress, a new used lathe, a wealthy and devoted client, a feeling of security, a sense of self-worth. But Freddy kissed me, and smiled his open-hearted, sexy smile. I told him we didn't need anything.

And then six months ago, a Tuesday, two P.M., Freddy's in Birmingham, on a round of cold-calls. I decide to quit early since I have no work to do—nothing at all—and on the way to our apartment I stop to buy a bottle of cheap wine, to artificially raise our spirits. Walking home from Ernesto's Party Shoppe, I'm struck by the beauty of the sun on the western wall of our apartment building, the way the aluminum siding is draped in hazy, honey-colored light. I open the door. Freddy is lying on the sofa in his suit pants, watching *Oprah,* his hair a carroty scrawl on the cushion. A smell of marijuana hangs in the air.

"What's wrong?" I ask him. "Why aren't you out on calls?"

Freddy sits up, startled, and clicks off the TV. "Well, yes, I was going to go out this morning," he says. "I was planning on heading to Birmingham, to some of those jewelry places. But, then ... I didn't go."

"Why *not*, Fred? Are you okay?"

Freddy nods.

I slump on the sofa in disbelief. "When's the last time you went out on calls?"

He frowns deeply, as if he hasn't understood the question. Finally he says, "I guess it's been a while."

That afternoon we sit at the kitchen table sipping cheap Merlot from coffee mugs, while Freddy explains that he hates the emptiness of it, selling a product people don't really *need*, and that when he's working a pitch, he sometimes feels a deep burning, like an ulcer, at the bottom of his stomach. He hates the vague sense of dishonor associated with convincing people to give him money. And finally, Freddy says, selecting his words carefully, he doesn't necessarily mind failing. There's a bitter rightness in failure.

"We lost my car, Freddy! I *liked* that car!"

"Yes, okay, I realize that," he says, his voice rising. "Maybe, I don't know—maybe the mannequin concept just isn't meant to be. I've been thinking about new ideas these last few weeks. Are you ready?" He leans over the table and spreads his hands wide, framing a scene like a movie director. "Picture this: wooden shoes. Hand-carved soles, hand-dyed leather uppers. Picture every college kid from Grand Rapids to Port Huron wearing our clogs."

"Let me get this straight," I say. "You've been smoking pot and dreaming about clogs for the past few weeks? And then coming down to the shop and *pretending* you were out on calls?"

I try to remain civilized. I can't do it. I call him a dreamer, an idiot, a shit-sucking liar. Freddy slaps me once, hard, above my right eyebrow. Immediately I'm facedown on the kitchen floor and Freddy's on top of me, kissing the side of my face, crying. Lying there, on the floor of our terrible apartment, I remember the hazy sunlight of that afternoon, and a painful twinge of happiness arches through me. What sunlight! My whole life seems justified by that patch of light! Freddy's whispering phrases I can't understand; I hear only a high-pitched pink noise that eventually fades to nothing. Freddy weeps silently.

There is much injustice in the world, according to Freddy, that no one wants to talk about. I'd tend to agree with him. But that afternoon he didn't feed me his usual excuses; he told me the truth. Why am I such a sucker for the truth? That night, like every night, I slept next to him on our silt-stained mattress. The next morning, like every morning, I drank grapefruit juice with him at the kitchen table. And the next evening after dinner, like every evening after dinner, Freddy switched on the ten o'clock news and railed at poor Carmen Harlan, the beautiful anchor-woman, for her role in the spread of misinformation. It's his way of relaxing, the way some people play dominoes, or raise exotic fish.

But as I watched him sitting in front of the television, taunting Ms. Harlan, glancing at me with an encouraging smile, I didn't smile back. I know you, I wanted to say, so don't talk to me about misinformation. Don't talk to me about injustice.

I follow Freddy across Main, past the sidewalk bench where my reconnaissance fell apart. I feel tingly and nervous, like I'm on the verge of something risky, and I like the feeling—it has a nice edge to it. It reminds me of being in the middle of a shouting crowd, on the steps of the Fleming administration building.

Kennison, the woman Freddy's supposed to meet, arrives five minutes after we sit down. We stand to shake her hand—she's in her thirties, tall, with brown hair and delicate, china-doll features. Her suit (a pink Chanel-esque number—short to the point of tartishness) looks like it cost more than my net worth. She is not unattractive. Freddy, in the middle of chewing a piece of buttered bread, swallows hugely and coughs.

"You're Freddy," she says. Her accent is mildly southern. "Well. You're different from what I imagined."

"People sometimes tell me that, because of my voice. They expect someone taller, I guess." He shrugs. "It used to bother me, from a self-esteem point of view, but it doesn't anymore."

Kennison smiles faintly. Freddy has taken off his suitcoat, and there are sweat wings seeping from the armpits of his pale blue shirt; he looks like he could flap his arms and achieve liftoff. My guess is that there's nothing he'd rather do right now: fly out of his seat, out of this restaurant, out of this suddenly uncomfortable and disappointing life. (Poor fella—I reach under the table and give his knee a reassuring squeeze.)

"So," I say. "You own a gun range."

"Yes," she says. "I own a target range, in Armada. My father owned one in Knoxville when I was a girl, and I opened shop in Armada about seven years ago. People usually find it surprising: little me running a range." She shrugs pleasantly. "It's the old story—daddy teaching his only daughter how to shoot. It's in my blood, I guess."

"My uncle tried to teach me how to shoot once, when I was seven," Freddy says. "Seven is a very early age to expose a child to hunting, in my opinion. The sheer violence of the weapons, and all the blood, the gutting . . ." He trails off. "Excuse me, I believe it's called *cleaning*."

"You're thinking of fishing," Kennison says. "You *clean* a fish. You *gut* a deer. You had it right the first time."

"He brought home a buck every fall for thirty-one years, until this past year. He died last August, of colon cancer."

Kennison and I stare blankly at Freddy, then I realize—the confessional approach.

"Well. I'm very sorry to hear that," Kennison says.

A moody silence settles over the table. Kennison glances from Freddy, to me, to her menu. Thankfully, a waiter appears. Kennison orders the breaded chicken cutlet and a Diet Coke, and I order the same. Freddy, worryingly, orders nothing.

"Have either of you ever been to a target range?" Kennison asks.

Freddy chuckles, "Oh, well, no. Not exactly. Neither of us."

"You should come up sometime. I'll get my daughter Faith to give you a lesson. And—who knows?—maybe it'll give you some ideas for your mannequins."

I watch Freddy take this in. He's arranging his water glass, turning it counterclockwise. Finally he places both palms flat on the table and says, "Okay, Mrs. Kennison, I think I need—"

"Freddy is . . . opposed," I blurt.

Kennison stares at me.

"Morally opposed. Somewhat."

"Oh." Kennison smiles politely, as if she hasn't heard me correctly. "I see. And . . . what does this mean? And what about you?"

"Well. Yes," I say. "Me too. In theory."

"In theory." She nods slowly. "Well, this is shaping up to be a waste of time, isn't it?" Kennison produces a pinched smile and looks around for the waiter, suddenly impatient. "Believe me, I know the rhetoric and statistics and all the other rigmarole. I've heard that song and dance a time or two." She glances at Freddy. "You know, Freddy, I had a feeling as soon as I saw you that this project wasn't going to work. No offense."

Freddy says, "Okay, wait. Hold on. No one's quoting any statistics, or any *rigmarole*. Let's not get carried away. Yes, okay, it's true that I'm somewhat morally opposed—that's not necessarily a problem! Let's talk about this, the guns part, more thoroughly. Let's, you know, get it out on the table." He is sweating profusely. He loosens his tie-dyed tie, then takes it off and sets it on the table in front of him. The three of us stare at it.

"Well. That's good." Kennison brightens. "You had me worried for a minute."

"Let me make sure I have this straight," I say. "You want to buy some dummies, dress them up, then blow them apart with rifles?"

"Essentially, yes," Kennison says, nodding.

"Does that seem at all weird to you?"

The waiter appears with our lunch. Kennison takes up a knife and cuts her chicken deliberately. "It's a curious thing. A lot of men out here—I don't know if you've noticed—are fascinated by the militia movement. The macho aspect of it, I guess, the outlaw independence. I see them at the range on a Monday evening, dressed head to toe in tiger-stripe camouflage. At a target range! And these aren't backwoods wackos—they're lawyers and pediatricians." She arches her plucked eyebrows. "A number of them have been pushing me to develop a 'scenario,' like an FBI training ground, with mannequins planted in gutted-out buildings and down narrow alleyways. They'd move through the scenario and shoot dummies as they came upon them." She sips her water and dabs the corner of her mouth with a napkin. "It's a little strange, yes."

Freddy leans forward over his plate. "Doesn't that bother you? You know, the bigger picture: promoting this violent, destructive behavior? I mean—wait, okay, I won't give you statistics, here's a case in point: my uncle, the one who took me hunting, used to make my aunt call him Captain. 'Here's your sandwich, Captain. Captain, your shoelace is untied.' He'd never even been in the army! And he continually threatened to kill his neighbor's Pekingese—I witnessed this, as a child."

Kennison ignores him. "We tested plastic mannequins, but they shattered too easily—anything above twenty-two caliber just tore them to pieces. I'm looking for something that can absorb impact. So, wood. Your mannequins seem perfect."

"Okay, wait," Freddy says. "Let's detour for one second. Maybe you could use our mannequins to *advertise* something for your business. See? Imagine: you walk in the door of your gun shop, and there are mannequins on your right and left, wearing the latest camouflage pants and vests and orange hats. I can guarantee increased movement on whatever you put on our mannequins. Judith and I could set up a display for you, a demo. We could do it this afternoon. We could do it right now, even."

"We don't sell gear," Kennison says. "Just ammunition."

"We could work something out for ammunition," Freddy insists.

Beneath the strain of pleading, his voice holds a thin note of anguish. Kennison, I think, hears it. She turns to him. "Have you ever fired a gun, Freddy? There's a split second while you're squeezing the trigger, just before the hammer releases, when your heart freezes. It stops completely, for that little instant. It's relaxing, in its own way." She smiles, as if she's recalling a particularly satisfying round. She seems to be enjoying this. "Freddy, are you okay? You look a little uncomfortable."

"I'm just very uncomfortable, in general."

"He's often uncomfortable," I say. "It's not a major problem."

"You're trembling," she says, and the three of us stare at Freddy's hand. It's doing a tiny vibrato on the tablecloth.

Kennison reaches across the table and covers his hand with her own. She says, "You'd make a terrible hunter, Freddy."

Traffic on Woodward is backed up behind an eighteen-wheeler hauling a load of cinder blocks. Our Volare, as if in tune to Freddy's mood, makes a loud groaning noise when he touches the gas. Freddy is hunched over the wheel, recounting the meeting's events with dread amazement.

Kennison loved our dummies. With the waiter's permission I cleared a small space near the table and assembled an androgynous adult-sized mannequin that I'd once upon a time named Gunter. I showed off Gunter's hardwood limbs and modular construction and articulated joints. Freddy looked on silently. Kennison sipped Diet Coke and jotted notes in her Franklin planner, and when I finished, she described a potential order so large, so impressive in its double-digit heft, that I stared at her for a long moment without saying anything. Is it *feasible,* she repeated slowly, speaking to me as if I were a child—could we deliver a trial group of sixteen dummies in two weeks? She was worried that we didn't have enough manpower. I told her we'd fax her a contract this afternoon. (And I told her we had plenty of womanpower.)

"She's a very disturbed individual," Freddy insists now. "Her body language, I mean—did you notice the way she used her knife? It was very aggressive. She was very aggressive with her cutlet."

"I kind of liked her," I say. "I thought she seemed fairly normal."

"Sure, normal—whatever that means. Personally, I don't want anything to do with that woman, or her gun range. She can shove it straight up her *rigmarole*." He glances critically at me. "You seemed right at home in there. Maybe we should switch jobs—you can drag that case around and try to convince people to buy stuff they don't want. You seem to have a knack."

"Someone had to do it. If I left it up to you, Fred, we'd be lying on the sofa watching *Oprah*, wearing wooden shoes! And you should seriously consider dropping that confessional approach. It freaks people out."

"It puts them off balance," he says. "That's what it's supposed to do."

Freddy cranks down the window and leans heavily on the sill. The small wrinkles at the corner of his eyes are new; so are the flecks of gray at his temples. A redhead going gray: it's an unnatural, tragic sight. I take out a cigarette, light it, and jet a satisfying stream of smoke out the passenger-side window. He's a pig, according to Tania—the only person I've told about the *Oprah* incident. A scumball. He's a dirtbag, and she's lost major, major respect for me. She's told me this a hundred times, stubbing out her Camel Light disgustedly, as if it were Freddy's face she was stubbing out. And yet Tania's never had a boyfriend. I talk to her about how I feel, I try to explain it using the only metaphors I know—woodworking—and she stares at me, blank as a quartersawn board.

"What about the original plan?" Freddy asks. "A little boutique with a loft upstairs? Making one-of-a-kind pieces, with real craftsmanship and detail? We have all that! We have the shop. We have our client list, which is sort of small, okay, but not bad." He reaches across the seat and squeezes my hand. "And I've been kicking around some new ideas. Think about this: individually jointed fingers. And I've been thinking about different woods, combinations of woods. A curled maple head on a cherry torso. Fruitwoods for the arms. Think of how beautiful that would be."

"Think of how expensive that would be."

He sighs. Traffic has stopped completely, and heat rises in shimmery tendrils from the Volare's hood. Freddy drops my hand and stares out the windshield, lips pursed. "Do you think I *like* all this? I mean, look at my clothes." He slaps his cheap suitcoat. "Look at my fucking suit."

"I'm looking."

"I hate it. You know what I think about these days? Capital equipment depreciation." He shoves a loose curl back from his face and grins bitterly. "That's me, mister depreciation."

"Who knows, Freddy?" I find myself saying, too loud. "Maybe we need a little time to think."

There's a stillness in the car, the stillness you sometimes feel after a thunderstorm. "What do you mean?" Freddy asks cautiously.

Part of me wants to tell him about the dreams, the ones with the army of mannequins and Nova X3000. Dreams of lathes: there's something inescapably strange and sad about it; it feels like the result of a wrong turn, a missed exit. If I believed in fate, as Freddy does, I'd tell myself there was no need to worry, that all things are predestined, that even the most unanticipated disappointments have purpose. But I don't believe in fate.

After a while I say, "I could use some time off."

Freddy takes this in. When the light changes, he makes a slow right and heads toward Grand River, away from home. He hangs a right on Elizabeth, a right on Cass, then we roll to a stop in front of Sally K designs. It's still there, standing in the shop window—the first mannequin we ever sold. It's wearing purple sunglasses and blue bathing trunks, flip-flops on its club feet. Even from thirty feet away I can see flaws in the potatolike head—my first head—and the difficult, knotted shoulder that reduced me to tears. Freddy slips the car into park, leans across the Volare's bench seat, and kisses me firmly on the lips. I'm too shocked to kiss him back. He pulls back and searches my face— grimly, the way a doctor examines a troubling X-ray—and I find myself holding my breath. Finally he turns back toward the mannequin. It's standing on a scatter of sand, beside a pink beach towel. Its rough wooden thighs look fittingly suntanned. It stares at us blankly, like a lifeguard surveying deep water.

The shop's temperature when we arrive is one hundred and four degrees: a feeling of wading through warm oil. Freddy throws open the corrugated-steel door and retreats to his air-conditioned office. I straighten my workbench, sweating, then polish my tools until the chisels and gouges gleam like surgical instruments. The chuck of my old Delta lathe is empty—it's been empty for two weeks, waiting for an order—and the sight of it gives me a cool electric thrill. Sixteen dummies.

I work restlessly on the rough-out of an arm until I see Freddy step from the office with his shirt untucked. He gives me the *going to get soda* sign and points outside, toward Ernesto's Party Shoppe. I nod. When he's gone I throw the lathe circuit breaker and unlock the office door. I flip on the computer and scan the disorganized hard drive until I find what looks like our standard contract. I type in Kennison's information from her business card and click "print," and the contract rolls halfway out of the printer, then jams. A yellow light blinks idiotically. I yank out the accordioned page, feed in a fresh sheet, click "print" again, and this time coax the contract out with tiny encouraging tugs. Why am I nervous? I expect Freddy at any moment to burst in and stare, openmouthed, at the incriminating document. With his faux–Mont Blanc I sign on the line labeled "Owner, Blockhead Mannequins," then dial Kennison's number on the fax machine and feed in the contract, praying silently to the god of electronic transmissions. Finally the machine beeps—transmission successful—and I feel a small tremor, like a sparrow has landed on my heart.

I'm back in the shop sanding the roughed-out arm when Freddy arrives with the soda. He makes his way to my workbench and pulls up a stool, and I cut power to the lathe. He hands me a bottle of Diet Coke, picks up an unfinished head from my workbench, and turns it over in his hands. Without looking at me he says, "You faxed Kennison the contract?"

I attempt a casual nod.

"I didn't think you would," he says. "I didn't think you knew how to work the fax machine."

I want to laugh, relieved, but Freddy's expression is impossible to pin down. Is that a hint of grin or not? His hair has straggled down past his eyes, and I can't be sure what he's looking at. With strange deliberateness he places the unfinished head in front of me. "I had an idea on the way to the party store," he says, without enthusiasm. "A new concept. Ready? Picture this: personalized mannequins. Picture my smiling face on all of our mannequins."

"I like it," I say carefully. "Let me work on it, Fred—let me carve a few models next week, after these Kennison dummies are finished."

"No. Tonight." His voice is a sudden chill in the heat of the workshop. "Right now, Judith. I want Kennison to see my face, when she's out on her shooting range. I want to give her something to aim at."

Without looking at him I fasten down a pair of bench dogs and clamp the head against the workbench. I select my sharpest carving knife. In the silence of our stifling workshop I carve delicate grooves into the soft pine, working away from my body, and soon I've uncovered the impression of a cleft chin, the bridge of a bumpy, beautiful nose. The shallow rise of an eye emerges, then another, then a comma-shaped scar in the right cheek.

"You're not looking at me," Freddy says softly. "Why aren't you looking at me?"

But I can't look at him; I keep my gaze fixed on the grainy, unfinished wood. There's a photograph I'm remembering, from a long time ago: the two of us sitting on the steps of the Rackham library on the morning of my graduation, me in a wrinkled black gown, Freddy in fatigue shorts and a faded blue T-shirt. My nose is sunburned. Freddy's orange hair tumbles down past his shoulders. We're squinting at the camera, expressionless, as if we know what is coming and are not afraid.

THE INDIAN AGENT

October 11, 1821

I ARRIVED at the Agency hungry and tired, and ill from passage on the *Toledo*. Last night we encountered a storm that tossed the boat like a thistle, and kept me awake with needling pains in my bowels and legs, which were soothed only by draughts of cold tea. When I finally slept, I dreamed of falling through a forest of thorny black trees. In all, a rather disturbing attack, and doubtless the result of excessive nervousness. I write this with a pair of gray flannel leggings wrapped around my head, to guard against cold and further illness.

A brief sketch of this barren place: a wooden-walled garrison of one hundred souls, huddled beside wide, rushing straits. The Agency (my new home) is a small rude cabin; wind sluices through chinks in the rough-hewn planks and sends loose papers fluttering to the floor. Already I have paced this room's length a hundred times. Natives are encamped nearby, and when I open the cabin door, I smell their cookfire smoke on the evening air. Are they Christians here? I have seen but a single small church—though the straits are called by both natives and whites *La Sault,* a diminutive of *Sault de Sainte Marie* (the Leap of Saint Mary).

Major Howe visited this evening, and recommended I begin dealing with the natives at once, and to be *wary of their ways.* I assume he means their reputed tendency toward lying and excessive drink. He warned me to beware temptation to pity their circumstances—to remember that they alone are responsible for their wretched predicament. They will exaggerate their suffering, he said, to secure gifts of food and tools. I asked Howe about an engraving I had seen in Detroit: human hair, scalp, &c. dangling from a curved war hatchet. Howe grinned queerly and did not respond.

Natives and half-breeds wander about—they are everywhere. I am afraid to leave this frigid cabin.

October 17

Temp. 44°. Finished Gallatin's *Synopsis of the Indian Tribes of America*; after the day's Agency business is finished, there is little to do but read. Most afternoons I stroll along the straits, to a grassy clearing where traders display their skins and colored blankets, and recline against a pine stump with my Psalter and a pipeful of Peerless. There is nothing of scientific interest in this austere landscape—and the natives seem to have progressed little beyond the lever and wheel.

After lunch yesterday a native entered the Agency clothed in a deerskin tunic and scarlet leggings. Seemed surprised to see me; accustomed to dealing with the departed Agent Dawson, no doubt. Introduced himself through the Agency translator, Joseph Montrè, as Ochipway. Claimed to be chief of the small band of Chippewa that lives along the Misery River (a peaceful tribe by all reports). Wanted to lodge a complaint against the settlers of Pickford, who had constructed a mill-dam on the Misery, causing flooding in the land where his people had farmed beans and pumpkins for many years. Said new attempts at farming had failed, and there would be hunger this winter. Said many members of his band were angry at the settlers and wanted *miigaadiwin* (strife, or great trouble).

Ochipway's appearance: tall for a native, and plump in a satisfying, masculine way, with a strong Roman nose and bluish-black hair that shines with the grease they smear over it to deter insects. His only defect is laziness in the right eye, giving an impression of uninterest, or boredom. Skin the color of moist beach sand.

Recorded his complaint and promised to confer with Major Howe. Ochipway, before he departed, requested a present of tobacco. I was somewhat taken aback, and recalled Major Howe's warning: that they will continually ask for petty gifts, and to be wary of appeasing them. Broke my plug and offered half. Ochipway apparently satisfied, yet strode away without a good-bye. Ochipway, meaning "Bird in Everlasting Flight."

October 19

Temp. 37°, with a clenching wind. Brought four letters to the post; it is ten days since the last delivery. My mind is restless—there are no inventions to rouse my curiosity, just natives and pine trees and the icy straits. Would sacrifice my good health for word from Detroit.

Many nights I dream of home, of the patent office. Macready reclines on the desk, wearing a native's buckskin leggings and moccasins; the furniture is broken to splinters; Jameson waltzes before me, like a woman, singing a bawdy lullaby. I have an unquenchable thirst. When I wake, chilled, I feel sick and disheartened. My soul feels weary.

October 23

Called at Howe's quarters this morning to find him upbraiding a young private. Apparently the man left the magazine unlocked, and someone (a native, assumedly) crept in and stole five horns of powder and a pair of rifles. Words repeated: *imbecile, idiot, treason, pity*. Spittle sprayed from Howe's lips and speckled the poor man's face and lapels.

A brief sketch of Major Howe: tall, white-haired, skin as burnished and creased as worn cowhide, with a prominent midsection despite slender arms and legs. Overall his body resembles a sweet potato. He is an intelligent man, and seems to regard everyone with cordial mistrust, bordering on condescension. His brother, according to rumor, was scalped by Chippewas during the River Raisin massacre.

Offered Gold Choice, which I gratefully accepted. Seated beside the stove, with rivulets of pipe smoke commingling above our heads, we discussed: tobacco rationing for the coming winter; modern methods of food preservation; mechanical principles of lithography; Shakespeare (*Richard II*). Finally I related the dispute between Ochipway's Chippewas and the settlers at Pickford. Howe removed his pipe from the corner of his mouth.

—No settlers have trespassed on reserved land, true?

–True.

–The treaty grants equal rights to the Misery, true?

–True.

Howe closed his eyes. For a moment, with tendrils of smoke curling about his face, he seemed the picture of a man at peace. –The natives complain continuously, despite receiving generous annuity payments. It strikes me as ungrateful.

Told Howe I believed the natives felt the flooding violates the *spirit* of the treaty. Howe interjected. –The treaty has no spirit, only words. If we allow for interpretation of "spirit," we risk severe unrest.

He cleared his throat and smiled, resting his hand on my forearm in an avuncular manner. –Our first responsibility is to American citizens, Hobart, not a ragged band of heathens. Sometimes in our pity we forget this.

I agreed. Suggested that perhaps I should attempt to negotiate a compromise, to ensure harmony. Howe snorted, a twin puff of smoke escaping through his nostrils, then coughed harshly. –You forget that natives cannot comprehend such logic. When dealing with natives, you must consider logic a native would follow; anything else is uncharitable. He regarded me, teary-eyed from his coughing spell. –We're at the fag end of creation, Hobart. I hope you've realized that.

Told him I had.

November 16

Temp. 31°. I feel solitary. As of last night's hard freeze, we are detached from the world—the season for navigating has closed. As the *Mary Elizabeth* prepared to depart, I had a frantic urge to rush from this cabin with only the boots on my feet, and stow away. Instead took an ax and chopped a large maple into billets. Work, at times like this, is a sweet mercy: it allows a man to forget anything, even his true self.

To divert myself, have begun a comprehensive study of the Chippewa people—their language, character, and customs. Read in Spurzheim a phrenological assessment of the native: *Distinguishing marks of the Indian skull are large regions of Destructiveness, Cautiousness, and Secretiveness, while the perceptive faculties—Hope, Spirituality, Conscientiousness, and Ideality— are moderate or small. In character, the American Indian is brave, cunning, cruel, lazy, revengeful, and unrelenting. His powers of abstract reasoning are small, and the range of his mind very limited.*

Agree partially with Spurzheim's judgments: natives seem to feel no guilt at indolence, no compulsion for sustained work. When morning fishing has been plentiful, you find braves sprawled along the beach like driftwood. Laziness, gluttony, drunkenness, godlessness: these sins are common in native life.

And yet, have found evidence to belie Spurzheim's generalities, most recently a discussion with a chief named Sagitondowa about native mythology. He related a half-dozen outlandish, brilliant tales; in the most fascinating story a brave fleeing a hungry bear transformed into a hare, then an elk, then an arrow, then finally a ray of sunshine that soared above the forest treetops and burst into an arc of radiant color. This, Sagitondowa claimed, is the origin of the rainbow.

Related the story of God's covenant with Noah—our own divine rainbow. Sagitondowa silently thoughtful. Who would have thought savages would possess such imagination? There is evidence of intellect in the native race; it is baffling and piteous to see them helpless, in want of gunpowder and iron tools.

November 29

Ochipway entered the Agency this morning before I had shaved or taken breakfast. He was dressed in a heavy tunic and leggings, for winter, and a bright green *capot* in the manner of a French Canadian *voyageur*. Was limping slightly—unsurprising, considering the jeopardous nature of savage life.

I invited him to sit. He declined; stood before my desk with his strong hands clasped. Inquired about my meeting with Major Howe. Informed him that the treaty signed at Fond du Lac granted the Misery to both whites and Indians. That the settlers were allowed to build a mill-dam, but that it would be broken next year, when the timber was cut. Proposed that Ochipway's tribe temporarily farm farther south, below the flooded region, since there was much fertile land along the Misery.

Ochipway stared at me until I could no longer hold his gaze. Finally spoke a long, patient stream of syllables. Montrè watched, his lips moving slightly, and when the native finally stopped, Montrè spoke.

—He says you have broken the words of the treaty council. He says settlers have heightened the dam, and the spring flooding will be greater than before. He says his people are angry and mistrustful of you and the Great Father. Says words are like mud in your mouth, and you sound like the other one when you speak.

—Who?

—Howe.

Ochipway crossed his arms, his posture that of the *defiant red man* of engravings—and for the first time in weeks I felt a trickle of fear. Began explaining that it seems reasonable to expect his band to relocate their farmland, as there are two score settlers but only fifteen Chippewas. Stopped before I'd completed my statement. Told Ochipway I would consider the matter further. Told him to return after the first thaw.

Ochipway said he would report my message but feared there would be *miigaadiwin*. Spoke slowly, his voice tinged with bitterness. Does he mean his words as a threat? Or is he merely frustrated? Ochipway turned to depart; I offered tobacco and rations, which he accepted.

December 12

Thick snow, churning wind—cold. Temp. 24°. A sermon on man's equality before God but the necessity of faith to achieve salvation. A mail sled arrived last night, bringing Detroit dates of November 15th and New York dates a week earlier.

Issued to Oshawano and his wife six rations.

Meesho appeared at the Agency and said, —My father, I am cold and hungry, without even a cloth to cover myself. Have mercy on me. (Twelve rations and a two-point blanket.)

Saganosh applied for an ax, claiming his had been stolen. Charged him with selling it for ardent spirits; he swore it was stolen while he was hunting. Issued an ax, insisting he care for it better than his last, then lectured him on construction technique of a simple trout seine. (Seven rations.) Later he reappeared with a gift of three fine muskrat traps. (Seven more rations.)

An ashamed Caubamossa appeared; his injured leg prevented him from hunting for his family. Issued an awl, fire-steel and flint, twenty rations. A strangely somber native—finally admitted that he feared his *manito,* or watchful spirit, had abandoned him. Five more rations and a Chippewa translation of the Bible.

December 25

Christmas. Purchased for myself a sugared tea cake, but discounting this there is nothing to mark the occasion. No letters from Macready or Jameson. No dinner or party invitations. Temp. 7°. All glory to Him on this joyous day.

Dined yesterday with Major Howe and his wife Charlotte at the garrison headquarters, a stiff, frigid place with an utter lack of color. For furnishing the major has no shortage of fine things—carved oak newel posts, a pair of handsome Boston rockers, blue silk wallpaper overlaid with a delicate print—but they are arranged with complete disregard for beauty or harmony.

Charlotte: a tall, pale woman with the warmth of a whitefish. Easy to imagine her, eyes downcast, dining across from Howe every evening. Picking at her salt pork and potato, awaiting her husband's grunt of approval. Agony. The woman, when she rose to fetch dessert, lost hold of a saucer and sent it crashing to the floor.

Howe, after his fourth measure of port, related the story of a white man, Tanner, who was captured by Saginaw Chippewas as a boy and raised as an Indian brave. –He grew to manhood learning to hunt and fish as a native—quite remarkable, actually—and professed belief in their fanciful superstitions. At some point he decided to return to the white world, but his habits were so savage he could not tolerate civilization.

Howe sipped his port and shrugged bemusedly. –I met him at the Fort Worth Agency some years ago. It was the damnedest sight: he would not smile. He would not eat common food. He spoke English reluctantly, and then like an idiot child. Then one morning, unprovoked, he shot a white lieutenant through the throat and fled back to the woods.

Howe leaned forward in his rocker. —They later found the musket he'd used. The wad was a torn page from a hymn book.

Conversation drifted toward Agency business, in particular my expenditures on sundry goods (too great). Related details of Ochipway's renewed complaint. Howe shook his head, in the manner of a mother scolding an infant for a naughty deed. —This, three weeks after an annuity payment. Such is the result of your compromise, eh?

He chuckled, pouring another measure of port. —Give them corn, Hobart. Give them flour and rice. Don't let them starve, for mercy's sake.

Trudged home through a squall feeling inexplicably irritated—at Howe, and at myself. Would have kicked a spaniel, given a chance.

January 11, 1822

I never realized there are so many forms of loneliness. Yet the longer I am here, the more ably I can differentiate between the impatient loneliness of a Friday evening without callers, the despairing loneliness of a snowed-in Sunday, the hard sober loneliness of a Monday morning in the empty Agency. Each has its own bittersweet savor. Would sacrifice a month's pay for a weekend with Macready or Jameson.

Find myself thinking frequently of Ochipway. He is young for a chief, but possesses a chief's characteristically impassive demeanor; beneath it, though, he seems worried, or discouraged. His great gift seems to be an ability to remain calm where others would become irate (when dealing with Howe, for example). So few men understand the virtue of patience; what a surprise to find such patience in a savage. Fine, strong legs.

January 24

Temp. 9°. Sent for Montrè and a *voyageur* named Cloutier at sunrise. We boarded a *traineau* dragged by a team of half-feral Eskimo dogs, Cloutier urging the lead dog with cries of *Mouche!* or cursing it as a *Sacré chien mort!* The sled coursed up the frozen Misery. We heard deer crashing through the icy brush, and the woodpeckers' *rat-tok-tok-tok,* and the occasional cry of the lynx: a long, high keening, like a child in pain.

Passed Ochipway's village just before noon. The dome-shaped huts blended so neatly with the surrounding pines that I might have overlooked them, if not for the threads of smoke curling from each lodge. I strained to detect some sign of activity, but there was none. Cloutier's hoarse, rhythmic shouting was the only sound on the river.

Seventy yards upstream on the opposite bank was Pickford, a dozen split-log cabins in a beaten-back clearing. Timber is the reason for this place: a concern from Boston has established a sawmill farther down the Misery, and the men of Pickford are engaged in cutting white pine. We lashed the dogs to a birch and made our way to the timber office, ignoring the stares of four cow-eyed women packing snow into tin basins. Inside, a russet-haired man leaned over a ledger at a low table, a clay pipe clamped in his mouth. Didn't look up when we entered. Only after I'd introduced myself as an agent from the United States Bureau of Indian Affairs did he set down his pen and consider us.

—The savages across the river have been acting wrathy.

I wondered: how long does it take a man, separated from civilization, to lose the gentlemanly part of his character? And do his mental abilities similarly decay? The thought struck me that I, too, must be degenerating with each passing day.

The man stood and introduced himself as John Toomey. Eyed Montrè and Cloutier. —They're huffed about the dam. They stand across the river with their hunting spears, scaring the women.

—They're unhappy because the dam has flooded their farmland. There's a treaty, signed last year at Fond du Lac. It grants the Chippewas full rights to the opposite bank.

—And that tall one, he means to make trouble. He's savage as a meat ax.

Toomey removed the pipe from his mouth and spat between his feet. His hand trembled as he replaced the pipe, and it occurred to me that he was nervous—and probably terrified of the natives, as I was during my first days at the garrison.

—The tall one is their chief. He's registered a complaint with the Agency, and as agent for Indian affairs—

Toomey interrupted. —My wife's afraid to leave the cabin. She's afraid that tall savage will cut her scalp off. She has dreams about it.

—Mr. Toomey, I said, looking him in the eye, —those Chippewas are a peaceful band of natives. You have my word.

Toomey shifted his weight uncomfortably, avoiding my gaze. —Anyway, Agent Dawson told us to build the dam there, so you should trouble him, not me.

—Agent Dawson? When was this?

—Last September. So we built it. Just where he said we should.

Frowned at Toomey then at Montrè, who shook his head, perplexed.

—I want to register my own complaint against those savages. For being cussed. I want you to tell them to move on, just pick up and go.

Now Toomey stared at me, causing a flush to rise to my face.

—I'll need to review the matter with Major Howe. I turned and marched to the door, then turned back to Toomey. —And I'll need to verify your claim about Agent Dawson.

Toomey opened and closed his hands—a small, helpless gesture. —Just get those natives to move on. I don't care what you do.

Didn't linger in Pickford but set out immediately for the Sault; made eleven miles before being halted by darkness. Was exhausted from the sleigh's jolting ride, yet unable to sleep. Sat awake reading my Psalter by firelight. Found solace in the usual passages, in particular Psalm 137: *How shall we sing the Lord's song in a strange land?*

How indeed?

February 7

Something marvelous recently occurred. Kinwabekizze (Man of the Long Stone), a Sault half-breed and occasional drunkard, has built a church for the garrison's Presbyterian congregation. The building is small and bare, with a squat white steeple that can be seen far along the straits. To finance construction Kinwabekizze sold everything he owned, even the bed in which his children were born.

Applied for a shipment of four Norse mills from Detroit, at a cost of $108, in an attempt to improve native foodmaking technique. Reading Sterne's *Tristram Shandy* and Owen's *Analysis of Mechanical Devices*. Temp. 6°.

February 13

Spoke with Howe in his quarters about my recent trip to Pickford. Howe, drowsy from a lunch of venison sausage, boiled turnips, tea cake, and preserved whortleberries, hiccuped dyspeptically as I related Toomey's complaint and his news of Agent Dawson. —I'm tired of this squabble, Howe said when I'd finished. —We need only quiet the savages' grumbling for a few more seasons—until Pickford moves upriver. True?

—True.

—Fine. Issue them—he rubbed his eyes and frowned—twenty gills of whiskey, twenty horns of powder, five axes, two iron kettles, fifty pounds each of corn and pork. Then compose a declaration, requesting they temporarily move their farmland downriver—such formalities tend to soothe the native temper. He arched his eyebrows, in the manner of one quite satisfied with himself. —That should settle the matter.

—I pray it does.

—Tell me, Hobart, Howe said. —What does a man do without a wife in this desolate place? He smiled genially, a sight that sent a shiver through me. —What could possibly occupy a person?

—I read. I find enough in the Bible to fill even the longest days.

Howe stiffened. —Of course—although books can be cheerless companions. This is an arduous post, particularly for those who are naturally . . . *aloof*. He relaxed into his chair and regarded me with supreme indifference. —Would you like to dine with my wife and me tonight? We will have beef, and . . . what is it—that dish the half-breeds are so fond of? Ah! *Penishiquay.* Quite tasty.

Told him I'd be delighted. May the Lord grant me patience.

March 2

Cold, cold—temp. 22°. Even into March this peninsula strug-
gles against the notion of spring. Last night I witnessed a rac-
coon, half insane with hunger, attempt to climb through my
closed bedroom window. The poor beast scratched against the
pane then fell with a thump into the packed snow. Left a prune
outside, to keep him alive.

Ochipway called at the Agency this morning; seeing him
standing in the doorway, after months of absence, stirred a
pleasant anxiousness inside me. His face held a sallow cast, and
I bade him sit while I warmed a kettle for tea. Ochipway sipped
the steaming tea in silence. Such silence! The silence of a native
is as absolute and inscrutable as midnight in a forest. Only after
he'd emptied his cup did he ask, –Did you speak with Howe?
The river will thaw soon.

Told of my journey to Pickford and encounter with John
Toomey. Ochipway frowned in recognition as I described the
man. Told him I had spoken with Howe and been assured the
whites would remove the dam. Told him of the food and tools
we would present his tribe. Ochipway seemed relieved, his grim
visage easing into a near-smile. Produced tobacco and we
smoked. Smoked until the cabin shimmered before my eyes.

Before he left, I presented Ochipway with tobacco, powder
and shot, and six rations. Accepted all and requested six addi-
tional rations, explaining that his children were starving.

March 14

Awoke with a croup. As of today, my first priority is to get away
from this place—I am unfit for solitary life. This post requires

diplomacy and keen perception, rather than my meager scientific curiosity. Temp. 36°. Snow. There is not a single fruit or vegetable to be found in Sault de Sainte Marie.

Received a letter from Sub-Agent Thacker, who writes: *We have erred in encouraging Settlers to move onto land occupied by Putawatamies, who have protested peacefully but strongly, despite much abuse, including the slaughter of six of their horses by deceitful Whites.* He recommends a strategy of increased rifle sales to the natives, followed by elimination of our supply of powder and shot until acceptable treaty terms can be met.

Have begun assembling a rudimentary primer of the Chippewa language. *Oniẓhishin* is Good. *Maanaadad* is Bad. *Maanaadiẓi* is Ugly. *Mashkawiẓii* is Strong. Their sentences, I've noticed, have a certain rhythmical beauty, as one hears in the speech of those more civilized.

Giẓhe-manidoo ninẓaagi'aa: I love God.

Mino-ayaa debenjiged: The Lord is good.

Gii-kiẓhewaadiẓi noosiban: My father was a good man.

April 1

A white settler has died in Pickford. The man, Henry Harris, was found drowned in the half-thawed Misery, his body entangled in a thicket of willow. He was a sawyer by trade, and it is unclear what he was doing near the river...bathing in the frigid spring runoff? There are rumors surfacing that Harris was killed by a native. Much of this talk owes to a Pickford woman's claim that she heard a desperate cry on the afternoon of Harris's death.

Why would the natives kill one man—anonymously, at that? It is possible, of course, but on balance seems unlikely. More probably Harris died accidentally, but the settlers (Toomey) are primed to attribute any misfortune to Ochipway's Chippewas. Their frightened nervousness makes me uneasy.

The body was discovered by Mozojeed (Moose's Tail). Mozojeed removed a bronze crucifix from Harris's swollen neck and walked to Pickford, where he delivered it to the first settler he encountered—Harris's widowed wife, who screamed.

April 3

Awoke to snow as high as the tops of my legs. Temp. 42°. Spoke with Ochipway at the Agency about Henry Harris; Ochipway strenuous in disagreement. —The whites get drunk and fall into the river. This one, we see him fall many times: he doesn't swim, he nearly drowns. He is *gaagiibaadizi* (foolish). Ochipway stood with shoulders slumped, a troubled scowl on his face. Declined tea I offered.

I have no skill in determining when natives are lying—but Ochipway exhibited strange anxiety, continuously worrying the hem of his tunic. His lazy right eye was calm, but his left darted about the room. Offered rations and powder, which he silently accepted.

April 5

Rumor increases that Harris was killed by Mozojeed. Supposedly Harris was cutting brush near the Misery and was stalked by a stealthy Mozojeed and throttled. For what gain? None can say; Harris would have carried nothing of value, excepting his ten-penny crucifix, which Mozojeed admits to removing from the body. Harris's bloated, drowned state resists physical proof or disproof of death by strangulation.

To compound the settlers' unease, news has reached Pickford of the recent murder in Lac du Flambeau: a white settler was killed by a brave with a tomahawk, his skull crushed and brains strewn about the cabin floor, in front of his wife and young boy. Revenge, apparently, was the motive.

I prayed this incident would pass without requiring my involvement, but it is clear I must act. Sent a missive to Toomey with a half-breed named Perrault, who was traveling to Pickford this morning. Wrote the following:

The United States Government joins the settlers of Pickford in mourning the tragic Death of Henry Harris. Be assured his Soul rests in eternal salvation. Beware Temptation to assign blame in what is surely a blameless accident. The Chippewas are your Peaceful Neighbors and mean you no ill will.

Behold, how Good and how Pleasant it is for brethren to dwell together in Unity!

This completed, composed a second missive to be read to Ochipway. A difficult task—transpositive languages, like the Chippewa, do not easily convey simple conversation.

Our Great Father the president is Strong and Just, and will honor the Treaty as his word. The white men of Pickford do not wish to raise the War club against you. Treat them as Brothers.

Behold, how Good and how Pleasant it is for brethren to dwell together in Unity!

Spent the afternoon with Forster's *History of Northern Voyages*—difficult to maintain concentration. Grackles have returned. Strange to hear their merry chorus.

April 6

Howe has ordered a detachment of soldiers to Pickford to pro-
tect the settlers. Received this news from Montrè; hurried immediately to Howe's quarters to find him bent over his writing
table. Asked if such action was perhaps inadvisable, as armed
soldiers might increase tension between the two groups.

—Absolute nonsense, he mumbled, not looking up from his
correspondence. —Would you have another Lac du Flambeau
on your conscience, Hobart? Another River Raisin? I won't
have it. Better to be prepared.

—Seems a dangerous preparation.

Now Howe fixed me with a forbidding stare. His hair was
clipped short in the manner of Julius Caesar, and his uniform was
spotless and fully buttoned—he looked the image of soldiery,
and despite myself I stiffened, like a young private at inspection.
—Your idiotic misunderstanding of the savages never ceases to
amaze me, Hobart. Sometimes I wonder if you're truly fit for
this post.

I remained silent.

—You seem to believe they are Christians, that they have
some notion of sin. Would you live unarmed beside a band of
angry savages? Of course not. Why, then, do you expect the
settlers to do so?

Howe was suddenly infuriated; a thick bluish vein pulsed in
his brow.

—Sickening. Cowardly and sickening. I won't stand it. I've
seen better men than you scalped by savages. I abso—

—Major Howe, please—I simply wondered if we were perhaps making too much of a guiltless accident.

Howe snorted—then seemed to give up, shaking his head

and staring at me with a look of plain pity. Turned back to his correspondence. –You are weak, Hobart.

I remained silent.

Later, wandering along the straits, I considered my inability to make strong judgments, as Howe does. It seems, at times, that certitude *in any form* is preferable to indecision—and that my indecision is somehow tied to my perpetual loneliness. Sat for a long hour on a stump reading aloud from my Psalter. No solace. Why has He invested in me such a weak spirit?

Hear, O Lord, when I cry with my voice: have mercy also upon me, and answer me.

April 7

Woke before sunrise and loaded a pack with two days' provisions, my Bible, a horn of powder, shot, and a pistol. Called at Montrè's cabin, expecting to wake him, but found the old *voyageur* smoking his pungent *kinnikinnic* and mending whitefish nets. By first light we'd canoed six miles up the newly thawed Misery. Stopped for breakfast of salt pork and biscuit then fell back to the paddles; reached Ochipway's village and Pickford by two.

Cookfire smoke hung low along the riverbank, giving Pickford an appearance of a mirage or opiatic vision. Landed the canoe near the mill-dam; the settlement was quiet but for a hammer's crisp rhythmic *thock*. At the timber office found a bearded stranger, not Toomey. Claimed Toomey was cruising timber and would be gone a considerable time. (Worked a plug of tobacco in his cheek as he spoke; I sensed he was lying completely.) Told him I would wait. He offered sleeping space on the floor, which I declined.

Outside, made camp near the Misery then sat on the bank, smoking. Ignored the mongrels that sniffed curiously at our boots. Farther south, two men hoed furrows into a plot of chocolate-colored soil; their faint conversation drifted upriver. In the village center, Howe's four soldiers had pitched camp and sat on split logs around a fire, playing cards, their rifles propped against a pine stump.

Told Montrè to remain at camp and approached the soldiers, my stomach taut with anxiety. Recognized two men; addressed one I knew to be a lieutenant.

—You're to return to the garrison. You're not needed here any longer.

He rose from the log, still holding his cards. —Major Howe ordered us to stay. We can't return.

The other soldiers had risen and were fixing me with bored stares. One man opened his tobacco pouch and fussily packed a pipe.

—I'm responsible for matters concerning the natives. Major Howe knows that. I glanced from one soldier to the next, holding their gaze then moving on. —I'll speak to him personally when I return.

—Well. I don't want to cross Major Howe. It's not a smart thing to do.

I nodded curtly. The young lieutenant shrugged and slowly buttoned his vest.

Waited while they broke camp and smothered the fire, then tramped to the river and shoved their Mackinaw boat into the current. Watched their departure with a dizzy, weightless feeling—relief, mingled with something like pride.

That evening sat down to a meal of salt pork, hard cracker, tea, and whiskey. The flavor of the pork was doubtless sweet-

ened by my high spirits; the meal tasted like one from a fine
Detroit hotel. Fell quickly asleep, due to the whiskey, but awoke
past midnight with a start at a loud aquatic sound—a fish leap-
ing, or a large animal entering the Misery. I sat up. In the cloud-
less moonlit night the woods were eerily illuminated, the birch
trees' white trunks glowing like long teeth, the smooth rocks at
the riverbank shining like *wampum* shells. Settled back into my
bedroll, and then I saw movement on the river: a trio of canoes
gliding toward Ochipway's village. The oarsmen must have
been unskilled, as heavy splash rose from the paddles. In the
moonlight the canoes seemed to float above the water's surface,
like apparitions.

I struggled to my feet, the night air a cold grip against my
skin, and ran toward the riverbank, stopped, ran back to camp,
and yanked Montrè's blanket from his sleeping body. Took up
my hat and stepped into trousers and grabbed the pistol. On the
Misery there appeared to be six men per canoe, dressed in natives' buckskin tunics but with settlers' closely cropped hair. As
I fumbled with my trouser buttons, a canoe landed at the opposite bank and a man stepped ashore. Watched the second and
third canoes land, the men slipping into knee-high water and
stealing onto the riverbank, then I shouted *Goshkoziyok!*
(Awaken!)—and cocked the pistol and raised it high above my
head and pulled the trigger.

The shot cracked over the water like a beaver slapping its tail
in a smooth pond, and before the echoes had died a barrage of
shots exploded from the opposite bank. There was a moment of
deafened silence, the wind and river seeming to pause, frozen—
then a second blast of explosions and a chorus of shouts and the
high, frightened wail of a child. Dogs on the Pickford side sent
up a howl; a flock of partridges burst from the woods; there was

a roar from a white man and a native alarm call that ended in a choked, liquid cough. A man shouted *Oh, lord, Jesus lord please,* his voice carrying cleanly across the river, then there was a sharp cracking sound, like a dried branch snapping in two.

I raced up the riverbank to find every boat gone, even the Agency canoe. Waded hip deep into the frigid Misery, straining toward the far bank, surrounded by a muddle of noise: thicket rustling, shouts of *Here!* and *Sanebaw!,* musket shots, an astonished gasp of a man in pain. A chalky swath of smoke hovered over the far bank. Stood in the river for what might have been a minute or an hour, until a tense silence emerged. My feet felt pierced by frozen needles. Stumbled to camp to find Montrè crouched behind a pine stump with his knife drawn. Smothered the fire then huddled next to him, thankful for the darkness, thankful he could not see my face. Placed my pistol on the stump before us and waited.

Sometime later the trio of canoes skimmed toward Pickford. The oarsmen were quieter now, their paddles whispering through the water; they landed twenty yards upstream from us. Two settlers, their heads lolled to the side, were carried bodily from a canoe. Four others limped as they waded ashore. Montrè and I watched from behind the stump as they disappeared into the village center. We listened as, one by one, plank doors opened and banged shut. An owl whooped—twice, then twice again—then fell silent.

April 8

We drifted down the Misery at dawn. Pickford quiet when we departed, the village tidy but for a crumpled tunic near the canoes. Decided not to await Toomey—the understanding passed silently between Montrè and me—out of uneasiness, bordering on fear.

Clouds skated in from the northwest and flung warm rain down upon us; Montrè quiet, no rowing *chanson*. Floated past Ochipway's village to find the dwellings torn down and not a soul in sight. As we passed the camp I looked for signs of life, but there were none, and no sound emanated from the neighboring woods, and no smoke rose from the fire pits. Reached the Agency late afternoon, to find a shipment of four Norse mills from Detroit—my feeble attempt to improve the natives' fate.

In my office, began composing a resignation letter to Howe, knowing I would lack the courage to explain myself in person, knowing I would leave the letter with Howe's subordinate and depart silently on the next ship, like a stowaway, like an insect. There was a knock at the door. Private Stickley, a pale youth of no more than nineteen. Soiled uniform, dried grayish clay beneath his fingernails. Stickley reported a skirmish between the settlers at Pickford and the Chippewa Indians encamped nearby. Reported that the settlers were fired upon with muskets during a fishing expedition, and returned fire. He drew a folded page from his breast pocket and read the following:

A native identified as Chianokwut, Lowering Cloud, was shot through the forehead and killed. A native identified as Image Stone was shot through the chest and legs and killed. A native known as Returning Cloud, armed with a hatchet, struck settler Stephen Mason in the forehead. Mason's skull was crushed, and he was killed. A native identified as Little Thunder was shot in the throat and killed. A native identified as Ochipway, Bird in Everlasting Flight, cracked the neck of settler William Brady with a rifle stock. Then Ochipway was shot in the head and chest and killed. In all, four natives and two settlers were killed.

Sent Stickley away without message. Before he departed, Stickley eyed my tobacco pouch; I broke a plug of Peerless and gave him half.

Lay down to sleep but could not. Daydreamed of Ochipway's handsome, weary face. Daydreamed of my own death, at the hand of Private Stickley.

April 9

Spring snow. Temp. 31°. Managed to avoid Howe this morning, by not answering his assault on the Agency door; surely he wants to clarify my role in the massacre. Later I was overcome by guilt and disgust, and fear. Instead of weeping or lying down, though, I forced myself to take up the half-finished resignation letter and place it in the stove fire.

I must face him today. Rumor has it he is infuriated, war-ready. I must face him, though he may curse or strike me. I must explain that we should be cautious and compassionate, Christian, that we should not be vengeful—for what can I do besides appeal to his charity? And who am I, if I fail to face him? Howe is a cold man, but he does possess faith. He does have a soul. I must face his wrath with strength and dignity. I must.

KINGDOM, ORDER, SPECIES

WHENEVER I'm dating a man I could maybe, possibly fall in love with, I read him this passage:

> *Rarely do trees bear perfect flowers, having both stamens and pistils as well as showy petals. Species in* Prunus, Tilia, *and* Robinia *do have perfect flowers, and these are insect-pollinated groups. However, all conifers and the majority of deciduous species are wind-pollinated. Some tree pollens (like some individuals) are irritants, and provoke unpleasant allergic reactions.*

The passage is from *Woody Plants of North America,* by J. Poole. I first read *Woody Plants* in Gainesville, Florida, in 1985: I was twenty-one years old, four months from graduation at UF, with dreamy hopes for my future but no concrete goals beyond food and affection. I fell in love. Trees possess springwood and heartwood and sapwood, buds and thorns and tendrils, seeds and pith—it seemed a miracle to me then, as it does now.

So I studied forestry. It was boring work, mostly, sitting in a cramped grad student office at the University of Vermont, analyzing stem cores and computing canopy closure and plotting bole diameter data, but I ignored forestry's mundane reality and instead focused on its romantic abstractions: the complex marriage of species and habitat; the mysterious beauty of Linnaean taxonomy: *Nyssa sylvatica, Cercis canadensis, Larix laricina*. Often, thumbing through *Woody Plants* for a field identification, I found myself wondering who J. Poole was: I imagine a gnomish man in a faded flannel shirt, lightly bearded, myopic, susceptible to fits of joy. When I attended my first forestry conference, jangly with nerves and dressed in a black pantsuit, as if for my own funeral, I asked several people, *Have you seen J. Poole?* I wanted him to autograph *Woody Plants*—I was too young to have any sense of professional shame—but no one had seen him in ten years. He'd published his book, a string of seminal papers, and then he'd disappeared.

After I finished my dissertation I took an assistant professorship at Maine, bought a beat-up Saab 900, moved into a semi-hip loft apartment, put my wolfhound Coleman to sleep, published a few mediocre papers, was denied tenure, and occasionally thought about J. Poole. I'd collected some disparate rumors: that he'd received his Ph.D. from the Michigan Engineering Institute, that he was a decent squash player, that he'd once called another researcher "shit brain" at a crowded colloquium in Vancouver. This last anecdote didn't diminish my admiration (intelligence, after all, is often smudged with irascibility): in every office I've worked, *Woody Plants* has stood on the corner of my desk. The spine has fractured, and the cover's been corrugated by New England rain, but my scrawled marginalia and lemon highlighting are still crisp after fourteen years. Leafing through it evokes vague surges of memory; it's like looking at a scrapbook from a previous life.

I hadn't thought about Poole in several months, until today's lunchtime conversation turned to a book that's supposed to replace *Woody Plants* as the standard undergraduate text. Three of us are sitting around a battered pine table in a faux-Irish pub, in Slaney, Michigan, on lunch break from the North American Agroforestry Research Conference: myself, Henry Watt (a colleague from Maine), and David something, an associate professor at the Institute. David's drinking Coke; Henry and I are drinking Guinness.

"It's Aaltonen, of course," David says. "And supposedly he's publishing another book next year, on forest ecology. Have you seen him lately? He's developed a tic—the man literally twitches. He's like a squirrel."

"They're all that way, the Finns," Henry says. He's spearing French fries with his fork, frowning while he chews. Henry speaks in a loud, overenunciated manner, like a low-grade news anchor, and tends to grow vulgar after two drinks. For some reason he's always favored me—probably because I'm the department's only faculty member with breasts. "Overly ambitious, I mean. The weather must be horrific in Finland—they all work themselves stiff! Or twitchy, in our friend Aaltonen's case."

"Does Poole plan on revising *Woody Plants*?" I ask. "It'd be a shame if it went out of print."

"Well, I doubt it'll go out of *print*," David says. "It's a minor classic. Emphasis on *minor*."

David's an obvious admirer of Henry's (Henry is moderately famous), but his bitchy derision feels counterfeit, whereas Henry's nastiness is authentic. David's handsome but gangly, with a folded awkwardness that makes him look too large, I imagine, for whatever room he's in. He's wearing a maroon polo shirt and chinos—an improvement on the conference uniform of jeans and a crusty wool sweater. "When his book came out, I remember, Poole walked around the Institute like he was hot shit." His smile is both merry and dismissive. "Then he quit, or got fired, or something. Not such hot shit."

"I heard he quit because his wife moved to Mexico with another woman. She switched teams, so to speak." Henry waggles his eyebrows. "Poor Poole had something of a meltdown."

"To *Woody Plants,* and ambition," David says, a mock toast.

I arrived in Michigan this morning, on a twin-prop that left me nauseated and deafened on the tarmac in Houghton. The rental car lot is seventy-two miles from the Institute—seventy-two miles along Keewenaw Bay and through Ottawa National Forest, a lofty, silent sanctuary of quaking aspen and sugar maple and balsam fir—and when I arrived at the Slaney Sheraton I was riding a brisk high, which faded as I stepped into the lobby.

Forestry conferences are all the same: two hundred men (and a few women) in a high-schoolish setting of cliques, dirty jokes, and liquor. They remind me of the things I dislike about forestry—the backbiting, the prosaic triviality of most of the research—although twice I've listened to presentations that I immediately realized were breakthroughs. At those moments my boredom effervesced into tingly delight, and the room became filled with a gleeful feeling of shared obsession: we were like a group of nerdy kids huddled around a microscope, in an empty classroom, long after the other children had gone home.

"How well did you know Poole?" I ask David.

He shrugs. "Not well. He defended his dissertation two

weeks after I began. He was pretty aloof—everyone called him Woody behind his back. It wasn't a friendly nickname."

"I've tried to contact him a few times. Once I sent a letter care of the *Journal of Applied Forestry*—I had a question about his methodology in some biomass estimation work. No response." (I don't mention the two other letters, via different journals, or the telephone call to the publisher of *Woody Plants*. Or the idle fantasies about me and Poole sitting down to dinner in a shadowy cabin, in the middle of a snowy forest.)

"One of the emeritus professors was gossiping about him a few months ago. I think he still lives around here." David sips his Coke without taking his eyes off me. "I'll bet the department secretaries know where he is. Theoretically I could ask them."

I'm careful not to return David's stare. (I should admit that I've had a few sloppy moments at conferences.) "Let me know. I'd be curious to talk with him."

Henry glances at David then at me, a wry smirk on his face. "I sense impending fieldwork," he says, rising from his chair, "which means it's time for this elderly researcher to depart. Good-bye." He takes my hand and brings it lightly to his lips. "And good-bye."

The first man I read *Woody Plants* to was Martin. Martin was my first true boyfriend—my first mutual declaration of love, my first non-solo orgasm, my first shared apartment—and possessed a luminous, womanly beauty, a vulgar sense of humor, a mysterious affinity for insects, a way of watching me that made me nervous and happy. Martin was an aspiring mathematician. I was twenty-two, a rookie Ph.D. student, new to Vermont and postgraduate life. I owned a four-foot column of books, a diaphragm, no credit cards, no car, and I was in love—with Martin, with the Earth, and (yes) with myself. Each day seemed as though it'd been created specifically for my delight.

We ate take-out Indian, read secondhand novels, smoked Marlboro Lights, had sex. Martin liked to do it on the balcony of our third-floor apartment; one sweaty August night, after we'd finished, I tiptoed inside and returned with a candle and *Woody Plants*. I sat cross-legged and read in the syrupy candlelight. *Rarely do trees bear perfect flowers, having both stamens and pistils as well as showy petals*. Martin fanned himself with an empty cigarette carton. When I finished, he stared at me for a long moment. He said, "Are you done? I'm sweating my balls off."

It took me two years to realize that Martin was imperfect. (Even his incessant burping, I'd convinced myself, was endearing.) We never once worried about money—it was only *money*—then one day we ran out of money. Martin insisted I take out a loan, which I did (stupid, stupid girl). At the end, I gave him one week to find a new apartment, which led to a brief, ugly scene—a shattered fish tank, a bloody nose, a call to the Montpelier police—and then he was gone. And I swore I'd never again make love to a mathematician.

David's Bronco has smoke-gray windows and knobby tires; it's the sort of truck an adolescent boy would sketch in the margin of his algebra homework. We climb aboard, and David dons a pair of mirrored aviator shades (the international symbol of jackasshood), then accelerates onto M-28 into the shady beauty of Ottawa National Forest. Soon I'm feeling cool and vigorous, my mood dampened only by David's conversation: within twenty minutes he's revealed his undergraduate institution (Columbia), graduation distinction *(summa)*, the suburb in which he was raised (Grosse Pointe—Shores, not Woods), and made a veiled allusion to the size of his penis, by referring to his "thirteen double Es."

I share the following: that I attended a state university. That I grew up in Greeley, Colorado. That I, too, have substantial feet.

"I've read your regeneration work," I say, to change the subject. "I like the idea of comparing species within cladistic groups—it's an interesting approach."

"Someone at the DNR thinks so. As long as they don't cut my funding, I don't care. It's all about the money, honey." David grins, and when he sees that I'm not smiling, he nudges his sunglasses higher on his nose. "It's mostly restoration and management up here. Boring. For a while I was working on structure analysis with some genetics guys, but it crapped out."

I wait for David to ask about my work, but thankfully he doesn't. As a graduate student, I wanted my research to be a grand symphony of ideas—I'd explore all of forestry, all of botany, all of ecology—but even the tiniest problems, I soon found, are a maze of thorns. I swallowed my disappointment and plodded onward. Now my research lingers over a few narrow topics; I'm like a deranged pianist, repeating the same three-note melody.

"Why are you interested in talking to Poole?" David asks. We've passed from the forest into a scrubby, naked plain. Ramshackle shops border the highway: BAIT. EAT. "I've never heard of forestry groupies."

"I want to ask him why he quit. World-renowned researchers

don't usually just disappear," I say. "And yes, I plan on telling him how much I like his book. It's a good read."

"I suppose." He glances my way, inscrutable behind his shades. "Still, Kaye—it's primarily just a field guide."

True. But look at Poole on *Juglans nigra:*

A beautiful tree, but difficult to transplant due to its deep taproot. Squirrels often gather its seeds, bury them, and sometimes forget or lose them; this facilitates reproduction. A major caterpillar food of the lovely, pale green, long-tailed luna moth (Actias luna).

Then his next paragraph:

Terminal buds ovoid, silky-tomentose; 6 mm long; lateral buds 3 mm long, often superposed. Leaves alternate, pin-nately compound, 30–60 cm long. Petioles stout, pubescent. Flowers drooping, calyx 6-lobed; corolla 0; stamens numer-ous, with purple anthers. Wind-pollinated.

This is what I admire: the admixture of whimsy and preci-sion. Do we admire in others what we wish for in ourselves? (I lack any trace of whimsy, and possess only marginal precision.)

"Don't you ever enjoy something inexplicably?" I ask. "For example, those sunglasses?"

David smirks and clicks on the radio.

Poole's house sits at the end of a rutted logging road. It's nestled among towering black spruce and tamarack, and is made of hewed white cedar planks that must be three feet wide—old trees, older than me and J. Poole put together, older than the study of forestry. The house mingles with the surrounding forest so naturally that it looks like fortuitous deadfall. "And here we are," David says, killing the engine. *"Casa del recluso."*

I grab *Woody Plants* and surreptitiously smooth my eyebrows, then follow the slate path to the front door. The knocker is an iron fist against a tiny iron leaf. Silence, then padded footsteps.

He's smaller than I'd imagined, and clean shaven, with a hint of Jimmy Stewart around his eyes. A small gold hoop hangs from his left ear—a surprise, as is the blobby black tattoo on the side of his neck. He's wearing a clean gray sweatshirt and frayed jeans. His hair is clipped as close as a recruit's.

"Mr. Poole?" I can't help it, I'm grinning—cool, professional me.

He returns my grin but shakes his head. "You probably want the other Mr. Poole—I'm his brother, Brian. John's in Idaho."

"Oh." A speechless moment hangs between us. It's obvious, of course: Brian looks thirty-five, tops—too young for *Woody Plants*. "I was hoping to talk with him about his book."

"Sorry, I didn't catch your name." He smiles at David. "Or yours."

"I'm Kaye Lindermann. I'm a technical forester, and an admirer of Mr. Poole's—John's—work. I'm in Slaney for the agroforestry research conference and thought, well, maybe I'd drop by and introduce myself." (As I babble, I peer through the half-open door into the living room: red maple floors, a sofa draped with brown wool afghans, a fieldstone fireplace streaked with soot. Against the wall a wide cherry bookcase, elegantly half-full. Beside it, a framed juniper frond. Heaven.)

"I was in grad school with him," David says. His tone is less than enthusiastic.

"And you're ... his brother," I say.

"John's gone a lot. I watch his house."

Cumulus clouds were skulking on the horizon when we left Slaney, and now a soft belch of thunder accompanies the first pellets of rain. "I'd hoped to talk with him about his career. And there were some points in *Woody Plants* I wanted to discuss—semantic questions, mostly." A trace of disappointment has crept into my voice; to neutralize it I present Brian with my best Teflon smile. "Any idea when he'll be back?"

"I'm not sure—John's pretty tough to pin down." He squints up at the slate-gray sky. "I'd invite you guys in, but he's touchy about the house."

"Do you know what your brother's doing in Idaho? I mean, is he working?"

"I really don't know. Sorry." His tone is polite but firm. "I'll tell him you stopped by, though."

"One more question: do you know why your brother quit forestry?"

"John usually has reasons for the things he does."

Brian's smile is like wet cement hardening. Wonderful— I've offended J. Poole's kid brother. I've forgotten once again that in the real (as opposed to the scientific) world, women are not a novelty, and are therefore subject to rules of good conduct. "Maybe I'll swing by again," I say. "I'm in Slaney until Wednesday."

"Suit yourself," Brian says, already edging the door shut. " 'Bye now."

The second man I read *Woody Plants* to was Pavel. Pavel was Bulgarian, a legal theorist, a spectacular cook (and therefore a spectacular lover), with an infectious, easy smile and a tendency toward melancholy silence. I was twenty-eight with an embarrassing fear of thirty; I'd just finished my dissertation but felt profoundly less intelligent than when I'd begun. I had no job, no savings account, a blind Irish wolfhound, and a nagging sense that my real life should have begun long ago. Pavel was forty-two. When we met, his divorce was not yet complete; his wife's old black coat still hung in the hall closet.

We lived seven blocks apart in Montpelier. There was the matter of his selfishness, and shocking temper (in truth, I loved the idea of Pavel more than I loved Pavel himself), but I was starry-eyed: one morning I woke before dawn, and when I saw Pavel sleeping beside me, thin hair mussed and mouth peacefully slack, I thought, *So here you are. Finally.* I woke him and read from *Woody Plants*. The bedroom was half-dark, but I knew the passage well enough to recite it cold. When I'd finished, I glanced over: Pavel lay on his back, eyes closed, a faint whistle rising from his nose.

Pavel and I, together, possessed bad luck. We were sophisticated, careful adults—yet one drizzly Tuesday in October I realized I was pregnant. It hit me like an elbow in the gut. We talked, over lemongrass chicken and Perrier, and though we agreed on everything, there were bitter, shouted accusations. Our discussion ended with Pavel resting his chin in his hands on the kitchen table, utterly calm. He said, "You witless bitch." Four days later I walked from the Vermont Family Planning Center, past a single, sad-eyed picketer, and drove to an anonymous motel in St. Albans, where I stayed drunk for three straight days. And that was the end of my life in Montpelier.

Sunlight seeps around the Sheraton's armor-thick curtains at seven A.M. I roll over twice before I realize I'm alone—a relief, since the last thing I want is awkward chitchat with David. I shower and mix a mug of Folgers, then recline on the springy bed and try to reconstruct the night's events: returning with David to Slaney as the day's conference presentations were concluding; dinner with Henry, David, and a half-dozen others at some awful Italian *ristorante;* back to the Sheraton bar for a vodka tonic, then another, and another. And suddenly there I was: a thirty-five-year-old single woman, with mud-stained boots and cuffs, drunk in a hotel bar. Later, drying my hands in the ladies' room, I decided to sleep with David. I felt a jitter of nerves, but also a dull satisfaction, at finding a simple antidote to a wretched night.

Now, sipping coffee in my ratty blue bathrobe, I feel fatigued, hung over, and slightly gloomy—the morning-after cocktail of regret.

I throw on jeans and lipstick, then wander down to the mezzanine level and enter conference room B. A stooped, bearded man is genially discussing "Soil-Site Relations for Trembling Aspen in Northwest Ontario." At nine o'clock I listen to "Growth Response of *Pinus strobus* to Partial Hardwood Overstory Release," then a surprisingly absorbing "Composite and Calibration Estimation Following 3P Sampling." Afterward I duck into the ladies' room and splash cold water on my face, then walk a lap around the elevators to stretch. Then I settle into a chair overlooking the marbleized lobby, flip open my laptop, and click through backlogged e-mail.

As you know, your appointment as assistant professor will terminate on August 31 of this year.

It's from my department head, Gerald Haines.

We'd like to make your exit transition as smooth as possible. Would you please send me your available times next week to discuss administrative details (e.g. intellectual property, benefits, keys)? Many thanks for your assistance, Kaye!

Fuck.

"You look anxious."

David's standing in front of me, clutching a satchel in one hand and laptop case in the other. He's wearing a gray sweater with his conference nametag pinned to the chest, and grinning in a dopey, overfriendly way.

"Just a little depressed. E-mail about my career has that effect on me."

"Want a piece of useless advice?" He perches on the chair beside mine. "Care less. I mean, don't care so much about your 'career.' Try to find an interesting piece of research and grab it— if you're lucky, it'll distract you from the other garbage."

Is he serious? It's difficult to tell: his strained smile is neither earnest nor ironic. (A moment from last night flashes in my mind: after we'd finished, David rolled off the bed and staggered to the bathroom, and without closing the door he peed, long and loud. Even then, drunk, the act seemed awkwardly intimate; now the memory sends a flush to my cheeks.)

"I've been thinking about yesterday," I say. "Maybe Brian wasn't really Poole's brother."

David's grin wanes. "Who else would he be—his lover? I'm pretty sure Poole's straight."

"He was odd, though, wasn't he? Not inviting us into the house, getting annoyed with me for asking simple questions."

David's fingernails, I notice, are as torn and chewed-on as my own. "If he weren't so young, I'd say he might be John Poole—that he was bluffing, to get rid of us."

"I've met Poole, Kaye. And besides, foresters aren't exactly bluffing types."

True. Foresters are backgammon types.

"Anyway, he seemed reasonable to me. I wouldn't want a pair of scruffy strangers tramping through my house when I'm away."

"I wouldn't know," I say. "I rent."

"I heard a rumor once about Poole," David says, squinting in recollection. "Apparently, while he was a Ph.D. student, he went off to work in the woods, alone—somewhere in Ontonagon County, but no one knew where. Never told anyone where he went, never told anyone when he'd be back. He'd send his adviser a letter every few months, but that was it. Then one day, four years later, he showed up at the Institute with a four-hundred-page dissertation. And that was that."

I frown at David—yet beneath my skepticism I feel a flicker of pleasure. Alone in a forest, with a tent and data book, a skillet and theodolite and maybe a little Scotch. Talking to moss and stones instead of annoying academics. Knowing each tree as well as you know your sister. Could that be forestry?

"Listen, Kaye, do you want to grab lunch?"

David's leaning against the mezzanine railing, hands stuffed in his pockets like a schoolboy. (Last night his touch was unexpectedly soft, as though I were an overripe fruit he was afraid of bruising. It was too dark to see his face, but toward the end he uttered a groan that rose to a whimper, then fell to a soft, sighing cry.)

"I'd love to." Teflon smile. "But I really should catch up."

"No problem," he says, backing toward the elevators. "I'll see you later this afternoon. Or tonight."

"Tonight."

He ducks behind a row of artificial dogwoods, and he's gone.

Tuna salad from a dingy sandwich shop, a hackneyed keynote address, two catty panel discussions on selective defoliation, then up to the sixth floor, to my room, feeling as though I might shriek from restlessness. I throw on sweats and grunt to a soft-porn step aerobics show, then shower, mix a mug of coffee, and spend two hours outlining a desperate grant proposal. Then I glance outside and see that it's dark.

In the window, Slaney's white lights roll toward the horizon then abruptly stop, as if at the lip of a bowl; to the west lies the darkness of Ottawa National Forest, darker even than the night sky. A shiver races over me, for an unfamiliar forest is like an exotic country, with its own kings and customs, laws and wars. Ottawa is inhabited mostly by sugar maple, *Acer saccharum*, but even the plainest forest is bafflingly complex. (Why, I some-times wonder, do we bother with classification? These two trees are *Acer saccharum*—but one is hunched while the other towers. One is infested while the other blushes with health. Kingdom, order, species: as though an elaborate name could describe even the simplest living thing.)

The telephone rings: Henry Watt, amid the din of a crowd.

"Kaye!" he shouts. "I can barely hear you!"

"Hello, Henry. You sound drunk."

"*Inebriated*, Kaye! Not drunk!" He mumbles something unintelligible. "Won't you join us? We're at—where are we?—we're at McCann's."

At times Henry's showbiz voice and courtly manners have fooled me into imagining him as an interesting, respectable person. Then I remember a Friday afternoon four years ago, Henry sitting in my office, watching me with unnerving patience: "My dear little child," he'd said. "I could just screw you until you break."

"Not tonight," I say. "I'm tired."

"Kaye, dear." He shifts the phone, and suddenly his voice is husky and close. "There are certain *individuals* here who are anxious to see you. Are you working? Your dedication is despicable!"

"Goodnight, Henry."

"Kaye!" His voice drops. "In all seriousness—come out. You seem foggy lately. Like you could use a drink."

"Not tonight," I say again. "Goodnight, Henry."

I hang up.

I wash my face, floss, and climb into bed at 11:01, according to the clock radio's angry red display. Am I foggy? I don't feel foggier than usual; Henry's probably confusing fogginess with my everyday veil of denial. For years, I've disbelieved that the life I lived was actually mine—is this my cluttered apartment? Is this my mediocre career? Is this my shitty car?—as if, by disbelieving, my true life would suddenly and magnificently reveal itself. It hasn't happened yet. Still, I try.

The last man I read *Woody Plants* to was William. I was thirty-two, living in Bangor and working eighty-hour weeks at UM, in the midst of a disturbing bout of envy for my father's life (the same brown colonial for twenty-four years, the same job at General Electric for thirty; now the straight, wide fairway of retirement). William lived in New Haven. He was fifty-three, an oncologist, smart-mouthed, married with a teenage daughter; our relationship was furtive, infuriating, exhilarating.

I read to him in a hotel room in Boston overlooking the Charles River, in a musky bed, his gray-haired head resting in my lap. *Rarely do trees bear perfect flowers, having both stamens and pistils as well as showy petals.* William growled. "Stamens and pistils. Read on." I finished the passage, and for a few moments neither of us spoke. Later, after room service salmon and two whiskeys from the minibar, William stammered that it was too hard, that he was sick with guilt, that I was killing him. So he'd decided to leave his wife, to be with me.

I felt a guilty rush of joy. How can I explain William? We were like two people sharing dessert at the corner table in a restaurant, half drunk on wine but sober enough to talk about poetry. (Our relationship wasn't perfect, but it was far, far better than good enough.) I yanked him down to the bed and kissed him until he gasped. *Yes,* I said. *Be with me. Yes.*

That's the scene I've imagined, anyway. William never showed up at the hotel in Boston. He didn't talk stamens and pistils, didn't decide to dump his wife. I slept alone that night, fidgety with pent-up anticipation, then drove to Bangor in a teary rage, calling William a goddamned coward and myself a pathetic moron. At home, there was a message on my answering machine from William's wife (who'd known all along, I believe): William would not be joining me in Boston, she said. Not today, not tonight, not ever again. And she was right.

Wednesday morning is a mizzling gray film against the sixth-floor window. I shower, gulp coffee, and arrive at conference room C ten minutes before my presentation is to begin. "Light Gradient Partitioning Through Differential Seedling Mortality and Growth" is met with moody silence from the thirty-odd people in the audience; then a lone question: "Do you think your results could have been influenced by airborne pollutant effects?" As I'm answering, the door creaks open, and David slips in and takes a seat in the rearmost row of chairs.

"You should've come out last night," he says, after the presentation. We're standing near the podium, alone; other foresters are munching cherry-cheese Danish around the buffet table, their hair still damp from the shower. "Henry tried to determine how much Bushmills his liver could tolerate. It was an interesting sight."

David's overfriendly grin has vanished. His manner is polite but slightly aggrieved, like the victim of an overcharge at a supermarket.

"Sorry I missed it—I was catching up on work. Your career advice didn't help a whole lot."

"I told you it was useless." He sets his styrofoam cup on the podium, sloshing coffee over the side, then clasps his hands to hide his trembling fingers. "You sound like my ex-wife—she thought a sixty-hour week was a vacation. I don't think she set foot in a bar during the last five years of our marriage."

"Maybe she was more interested in working than drinking."

"It was more complicated than that." David's gazing out over the crowd, as if he's looking for someone. "You're flying out this afternoon?"

"At four. I thought I might drop by Poole's before I leave— maybe this time I can get Brian to call the cops."

"I'll drive you."

Why not? I wonder. But then: *Why?* He's edgy and impolite.

He's passionless about forestry—and, therefore, probably passionless about life. "It's okay. I remember how to find the house."

"What are you driving—a rented Lumina? Down a logging road?" He scoffs: *silly woman.* "You'll get stuck before you go twenty yards."

"It's a Neon, actually."

"Ten yards."

David's staring at me with a strange fusion of desire and annoyance. "Thanks, really, but I—"

"Listen: we'll drop off your car, head to Poole's, then I'll drive you back to the airport. It's not a big deal."

He takes his sunglasses from his pocket and taps them impatiently against his leg. Around David's eyes I see the same wrinkles that surround my own, wrinkles that will deepen to furrows with a little more age and worry. Who is he, anyway? A male, a divorcé, a Bronco-driver, a mirrored sunglasses–wearer. A lonely middle-aged forester—just like me.

"I could use a drive, Kaye. I'm tired of this conference."

"Seems like you were tired of it before you showed up."

"Maybe I was," he says. "I'll see you in the lobby."

The rain has stopped by the time I check out of the Sheraton, but purplish cumulus clouds loiter above the parking lot and a thick, mossy smell hangs in the air. I drive north on M-28, David's SUV looming in the rearview mirror, and at the Hancock airport I ditch the rented Neon and toss my garment bag into the Bronco's backseat. Then we're back on M-28, with an awkward silence between us. David's wearing his mirrored shades, even in the poststorm gloom.

"What if he's not home?" he asks, after we've cruised through the forest and are turning onto Poole's potholed road. "What if he's still in Idaho? Or picking up dry cleaning or something?"

"Then I won't meet him," I say. "Not a huge loss." As I say this, I realize that part of me *wants* Poole to be absent—then he'll maintain an air of mystery.

"This looks unpromising." The gravel driveway leading to Poole's house is empty of cars. David kills the Bronco's engine, and I grab *Woody Plants* and follow the slate path to the front door, my stomach skittering with nerves. I rap three times with the fist-shaped knocker. Silence. I rap three more times.

"No Poole," David says. "You could tack a note to the door. Give it a lipstick kiss—that'll get his attention."

I peer into the curtained front window, then step off the edge of the porch and tramp around back of the house, followed by David's bored "Kaye?" There's a row of four windows, divided by a sliding glass door. Dark curtains at each window block the view; it's as though he's cultivating mushrooms in there. I rap hollowly on the glass door, then tug at the handle. It slides open with an aspirated rush.

"Mr. Poole?" I lean forward and speak into the gap. "Hello? I'm Kaye Lindermann, looking for John Poole?"

I push aside the drapes and peer into Poole's living room. Dust particles swim above waxed red maple floors and a boxy sofa and a pine-stump coffee table; the sooty fieldstone fireplace gives the room a faint smoky smell. Branches tick and scratch against the windowpanes. I step inside and hold my breath. "Mr. Poole?" My voice sounds shrill in the empty house.

I scan the bookcase—Darwin and Linnaeus, two gilt-edged Audubons, a slew of Defoe—then set down my tattered *Woody Plants* and take a new-looking copy from the shelf. A crisp whiff of glue rises from the copyright page: first edition, 1982. I was a baffled eighteen-year-old in Gainesville, Florida. I shelve the book and tiptoe into the kitchen. A gleaming Gaggia espresso maker sits on the counter, below a rack of Mauviel pans. Expensive taste for a forester.

I peek into what looks like Poole's bedroom: a bed with a tousled black comforter, a half-filled water glass on the bedstand. The walls are painted brown, and the curtains are brown muslin, so that light seems to disappear as it enters the room. The dresser is bare save for a framed black-and-white photo of a woman—Poole's wife, or lover?—reclining against a sequoia, head cocked, staring at me with a frank, accusatory expression. I shut the door quickly and pad down the hallway, and with a jolt realize that I'm in J. Poole's study.

There's a desk with an ancient IBM, another desk covered with neat stacks of paper, two tall green file cabinets, and a bookcase jammed with journals and conference proceedings with yellow bookmarks sticking out like flags. I scan the topmost papers; columns of figures cover the pages, with no notation save for a title: *Sumter 9/84. Colville 1/87. Ottawa 2/92.* A warm knot twists in my stomach. I riffle through a stack of papers, but see no manuscript pages—they're probably on his computer, which is off.

I flip on the computer, then there's a thump on the front door and David's muffled "Kaye!" I kill the computer and dash to the sliding door and pull it shut behind me, run around the house, then slow to a saunter as I come around front, to see a black Suburban crunching to a stop on the gravel driveway. The driver's door opens, then John Poole steps down, carrying a brown grocery bag.

It's him, this time there's no mistake. He's a small man, with a tufty salt-and-pepper beard and owlish plastic-framed glasses, and he's wearing faded blue jeans and a denim shirt rolled to the elbows—the forester's tuxedo, as we called it in grad school. He's smoking a cigarette (which, for some reason, is shocking) and fixing David and me with a wary stare. He says, "Can I help you?"

"I'm Kaye Lindermann," I say, my heart thrumming, "from the University of Maine. I was here Monday—maybe your brother mentioned? It's great to finally meet you."

David offers his hand. "David Wallace. We met once at the Institute—in '84, just before you left. I studied with Christian Lang. Temperate silviculture."

Poole studies us for a moment, then drags on his cigarette and speaks through a mouthful of smoke. "I remember Lang," he says. "What happened to him? He's dead, yes?"

David nods. "He died of a stroke, eight years ago."

"Shame," Poole says. "He was a decent guy. And he had a good mind." He flicks his cigarette butt into the gravel and starts up the front walk. "So. What can I do for you?"

"I wanted to tell you how much I admire *Woody Plants*," I say. "I read it when I was an undergraduate, at Florida—I was an English major, so it was the first time I'd ever seen a leaf diagram. I loved the precision of your writing. And your descriptions: *Pinus strobus. Asimina triloba. Juglans nigra.*" A humid flush rises to my face. "I applied to Vermont a month after I read it. It was my first inspiration."

"That doesn't seem like the best way to choose a career. An undergraduate survey course would probably give a fairly skewed representation of forestry." Poole's voice is smoke-mellowed, thoughtful, but with an edge of impatience. "But I suppose it's better than taking one of those idiotic 'aptitude tests.' Or listening to some career counselor who's convinced we should all be lawyers."

"It's worked out well for me. I'm a lifer."

"Sounds like you're one of the lucky ones." He presents David and me with a dingy, thanks-but-no-thanks smile and rests his hand on the doorknob. "I'm glad you enjoyed reading my book. I enjoyed writing it."

"I was hoping we could talk about your career," I say. "If you don't mind. I'm so curious."

His key is already in the lock, but Poole's eyes glimmer with—what?—suspicion? Annoyance? "What do you want to know about my career?"

"I've always wondered why you quit forestry."

"Why on earth do you think I quit forestry?"

I smile, but Poole's frosty stare doesn't waver. "Well, your papers, your books—you stopped publishing in the early eighties. I've always been curious why."

For a brief, frozen moment I'm uncertain whether Poole will shout at me or laugh out loud; then a wide smile splits his face, and he chuckles noiselessly. I shoot David a glance.

"I didn't quit forestry!" Poole exclaims. "I quit the Institute! I quit academia, and all its bullshit, but I certainly didn't quit forestry."

"Oh," I say. "I see."

"I could march into your conference right now and give a thirty-minute seminar that concludes that water helps trees grow—and the audience would politely applaud. Yet if I were to stand up and ask a challenging question, or—heaven forbid!—accuse some fool of being wrong—well, then I'd get scolded by some half-wit department head." Poole leans toward me, as if he's offering a secret. "And you see, Ms. Lindermann, your presence here today illustrates something tragic: academics think that universities contain an entire world. That if you don't publish, or don't attend seminars, you don't exist."

I nod automatically.

"And I haven't even mentioned any of the garden-variety idiocies, such as watching the Institute hire Eskimos and transsexuals and other 'underrepresented minorities' to replace perfectly competent researchers. Do you want to know why I quit academia, Kaye? Because I'd begun to feel ridiculous. Like I was living in a world run by spoiled children."

Poole clears his throat, then shifts his groceries to his other arm. "I don't mean to be overly dramatic. I have a passion for research."

"I know," I say, "I see it in your writing."

He pulls a cigarette and Zippo from his shirt pocket and lights up in a single deft motion. Quitting academia: what a wonderful, grotesque notion. It's unfathomable to me, who's clung to my job like a life preserver. Like an anchor.

I say, "So you're still conducting research?"

"Oh, yes. Of course."

"Do you mind if I ask what you've been working on?"

A smile tugs at the corners of Poole's mouth. "A small book. A follow-up to *Woody Plants*, you might say."

My chest tightens, tingling.

"It's far from finished, I should admit—I'm still gathering data for some of the newer material. But I'm in no hurry."

I could help him, I realize. I'm unemployed, as of September—I could come to Slaney and measure bole diameters and collect stem cores, or code simulations, or crunch statistics. I could be a cheery but critical assistant, sipping mint tea while I questioned his assumptions and proofed his logic. I could edit drafty chapters in sweats and a T-shirt, snow piled halfway up the windows, a brisk fire snapping in the fieldstone fireplace.

Slow down, Kaye—one step at a time.

I say, "Mr. Poole, would you mind signing my book?"

"Of course." He unclips a fountain pen from his shirt pocket, and I reach into my raincoat—and that's when I realize that I've left my copy of *Woody Plants,* inscribed with my name and address, sitting on the bookshelf in John Poole's living room.

I say, "I don't seem to have my book."

Poole shrugs, a slight arch of his eyebrows, and slips the pen back into his pocket.

"I think I left it on your bookshelf."

His expression clouds. "What bookshelf?"

"In your house. I let myself in to use the bathroom, while I was waiting for you. I stopped to look at your books."

Poole scowls, as if I've told a terrible joke, then turns and stares across the sitting room at the cherry bookshelf, with its single unshelved book. He paces across the room and takes up the book. He opens the tattered cover.

An image flashes in my mind, of state troopers cruising down M-28, sirens howling—which evokes the pair of Montpelier policemen standing in my apartment, the night Martin left me with a bloody nose and shattered fish tank. I was twenty-two years old. Then I see myself listening to John Poole call me a criminal and a ridiculous academic, which merges with the shrill answering machine message left by William's wife, on the morning after our failed meeting in Boston, where she promised that I'd never, ever see her husband again.

He returns holding the book. "You were inside my house, today."

"I'm so, so sorry. I wanted to meet you, to tell you how much I love your book. And I wanted to ask you what you've been doing all these years, what you've been working on. And then you weren't home."

"I think this was just an enormous mistake," David says suddenly. "John, I had no idea what was happening. I want to make that clear."

"You were in my front room, looking at my books, this afternoon?"

Tears rush to my eyes, and I stare skyward and blink them away. What am I doing, crying like a schoolgirl on John Poole's porch? Part of me wants to run into the woods, ditch my laptop and garment bag, and disappear among the black spruce. What a joke: I'd be a failed forester, lost in a strange forest, in thunderstorm weather.

Poole uncaps his pen, folds back the book's cover, and hunches forward as he writes. His handwriting is blocky and clear, even upside down:

For Kaye Lindermann,

Lawless in the pursuit of knowledge.

John Poole
Slaney, Michigan

He offers me the book with a strange grin. "I've met a lot of obsessive academics, Kaye, but you're the first stalker. I can't decide whether or not to call the police. Stay for dinner—we'll discuss the situation."

I'm nodding before I've fully processed Poole's sentence. "Tonight?"

"Your flight leaves in forty minutes," David says.

"You can get the next one," Poole says. "Don't worry."

Don't worry! All my life I've told myself to not worry, and been wrong; how marvelous to hear the words from John Poole. An airiness lifts me, like my limbs are filled with helium, and an image flashes in my mind, of me and Poole lying together in the Ottawa National Forest, in the middle of a thunderstorm, drunk. His plastic-framed glasses are missing. Rainwater beads on my face.

"Kaye," David whispers. "I think you should go. This is strange."

Stranger things have happened, haven't they? Wind pollination, for example, has occurred at greater distances than Bangor to Slaney.

I say, "I would be delighted."

THE ORE MINER'S WIFE

THE man, a Cousin Jack, lost a hand in the explosion and bled to death before they could raise him to the surface. Niklas was working farther down the drift when the accident occurred. He heard the percussive rumble of the blast, and his mood lifted in anticipation: the blast meant his shift was nearly over. They blasted at the end of each shift to loosen rock for the next crew. He straightened, his back a hard knot of pain, and for a moment the mine seemed almost beautiful: particles of ore shimmered through yellow candlelight. Then he heard the pop of a lone powder charge. A hoarse shout. More shouts, and Niklas let his sledge fall and started up the dark drift, toward where the shouts were echoing.

They rushed past Niklas on their way to the shaft, two Swedes hauling the man's slack arms and a sweating Pole guiding his ankles like he was steering a wheelbarrow. Candles on their helmets flung shadows against the drift's walls. A blood-wet stain glistened on the man's ore-blackened jacket. They hustled toward the ladder, shouting anxious Swedish phrases, then slowly mounted the rusted rungs. The man would die, Niklas knew, before they reached the next drift. The feeling was like a cold stone in his stomach.

He squatted beside a pile of trap rock and tamped down a pipeful of tobacco, and smoked with his crewmates until he heard the steam whistle's low moan. There: now the entire town would know there had been an accident—nothing else caused the whistle to sound in the middle of a shift. Niklas imagined his wife, Milla, peering up the road toward the mine, hugging herself against the cold. She'd search for her husband, praying she wouldn't instead see a bespectacled, red-faced representative of the Majestic Mining Company. A bitter taste of bile rose in Niklas's throat, and he spat and started toward the shaft, to begin the long climb to the surface.

At home Milla was bent over a bowl of peeled turnips, her face flushed from the heat of the cast-iron stove in the small cabin. She wiped a damp tendril of hair from her forehead and attempted a smile.

Niklas set his cap and pail on the table and kissed his wife's cheek. It's warm in here, he said. Sit. Take a rest.

I heard the whistle, Milla said. I prayed you weren't hurt, and then a bird, one of those strange dark ones, landed on the sill. I thought it was . . . I didn't know. A sign.

A Cornish man, Niklas said. The powder exploded late, when he was too close. An accident.

Milla nodded. She gripped the paring knife, her hand trembling, then set it down. Tears on her cheeks shone like quicksilver.

It was the second death in their two months in Iron Harbor. Pray with me, she said. Please. We'll give thanks that you're safe.

Niklas followed Milla into the bedroom and knelt on the cold puncheon floor. Milla bowed her head and began the familiar recitations, but when Niklas closed his eyes, he saw the dying man's face: eyes frozen wide and mouth open, as though he desperately wanted to speak but could not form the words. Milla murmured the Lord's Prayer. Tomorrow would be the funeral, hushed except for sobs from the broken widow. After the funeral, while other miners were drinking flip and whiskey in Jacob Wright's saloon, Niklas would walk along the Pickerel River to where it churned into rapids, and spread his paper and brass ruler and compass on a flat-sawn stump and struggle against the theorem, his theorem. His mind drifted toward the river: swirling elliptical currents rushing white over slick black rocks. Arcs and parabolas spun and eddied through Niklas's mind, and he felt a glow of excitement beneath his fear and anxiety. The sensation calmed him. He bowed his head and held the river in his mind, and let his wife's soft voice wash over him.

They'd married on the morning of Milla's eighteenth birthday and boarded the *Independence,* bound for upper Michigan, four days later. Iron Harbor: the name spoke of ore glimmering everywhere, even in the harbor's icy depths, and there were stories of men pulling soft yellow limonite from the ground with their bare hands. The *Independence* was crowded with Swedes and other Finns and a group of pale, silent Germans, and Niklas and Milla huddled beneath a woolen quilt on the steerage deck and listened to the groan of the hull and the low, nervous conversation of the other passengers. Smoke from the first-class kitchen lingered over them. They'd brought food but felt continually hungry. They clung to each other beneath the quilt, and Milla's hands clenched every time the ship pitched into the jagged sea. Niklas fixed his gaze on the horizon, willing himself to be steady in front of this woman, his wife.

Iron Harbor lay on the leeward side of the Huron range, in the middle of an ore belt everyone hoped was a hundred miles long. Hills blocked the view inland; the town was surrounded by the Hurons and a low smoky sky and a bristle of timber lining the shore. A clutter of hastily erected stores bordered a single road, their signs a series of bright mysteries: *John Stevenson's. Chandler and Cooper. Mercantile.* Hogs snuffled in the gutters, their hides a mottled reddish-brown from the hematite-rich dirt. It was true: ore was everywhere, even in the streets.

That first morning in town Niklas stood in the office of the Majestic Mine's captain, a man named Prout. Prout wore a drained, angry expression and stooped when he walked, as though he were forever ducking beneath a drift's low support timbers. He sipped coffee from a tin cup and squinted at Niklas. You speak English?

Niklas stared at the man. Prout pointed at his ruined teeth. English. Yes?

Niklas nodded. Some. He pronounced the soft vowel carefully.

Prout pursed his lips. Ore's soft, see? Don't need to know nothing, only be smart. Hold the steel, your partners swing sledges. Load the shot, spool the fuse, walk away. See? Keep your candle lit, you're fine. Pay seven dollars a week.

What if rock falls? Niklas asked. He immediately wished he could take the words back, but they were out, plain.

Prout swished the coffee's dregs in his mouth and spat onto the floor. Rock wants to fall, he said. Keep out from under when it does.

Niklas nodded. His new canvas shirt was stiff against his skin. From outside the office a dull pounding echoed. Right, Prout said. Let's go. Time to work.

The first thing Niklas noticed about the mine was the damp: water slicked the shaft walls and hung in the air. It was warm in the mine, even in October, and as Niklas descended the chain of ladders, watching the shaft's pocked face spool past, he felt he was traveling down the throat of a sleeping animal. The mine's groans and tremors seemed to be the animal's nocturnal rumblings.

Down in the raise there was the plaintive ring of sledge against chisel, and there was darkness: the darkness seemed tangible, a thing itself, as dense and malleable as the ore they gouged out. Its thick presence surrounded Niklas. He hunched beneath a massive stull, eyes closed, listening to his heart's skittish throb. He drew a long breath and then another. He imagined himself lying in the gorse behind his father's house in Oulu, connecting the night's stars with curves and brilliant line segments; he imagined himself capturing a bright jumble of stars and flinging them against the high ceiling of the raise. When his breathing had settled, he opened his eyes and ventured slowly into the darkness, like a swimmer into frigid water.

That night he stepped into the company cabin to find his wife sitting at the sawbuck table. His face was a maroon-black mask of hematite. His joints were tugged loose by the eight-pound sledge. Milla looked up, bewildered, then rushed to

Niklas and threw her arms around his neck. Niklas buried his face in her hair, stroking the back of her neck, the way he'd soothed his father's hunting dogs when they'd had distemper. Finally he held her away from him. Her eyes searched his face with a desperate intensity that made Niklas wonder if she'd forgotten who he was.

Later, in bed, after Milla's breathing had deepened, Niklas slipped from beneath the quilt and paced across the frozen floorboards to the kitchen. He closed the door and lit a lamp and set it on the bare table. From beneath the sideboard he slid a chest, then reached into his nightshirt and withdrew a small key on a leather strap. He unlocked the chest and removed a sheaf of penny paper, a vial of ink, a set of pens, a long brass ruler, and a worn compass. He smoothed the paper against the table and closed his eyes, ignoring the blunt ache in his shoulders, and steered his mind toward the problem, his problem. Like all geometry it possessed great beauty, but its simplicity had first drawn Niklas:

Construct a square, equal in area to a given circle.

At times he imagined the solution as a brilliant orb, gleaming like native silver. When he closed his fist around the orb it disappeared, yet Niklas did not feel disappointed; instead he felt a curiously pleasant hunger.

He felt he understood the problem's point of weakness, and although it might require months of struggle, Niklas knew the problem was assailable. For that was how he viewed mathematics: as a war of attrition between the problem and his will, a long, tranquil siege. Niklas recognized in himself a minor gift for translating elaborate shapes into simple, precise descriptions, and although he hadn't studied mathematics in school, the cover of his *Cranston's Geometrical Primer* was stained black from the oils of his fingers. The pages were worn as smooth as skin.

He covered the paper with line segments and arcs and scrawled Greek notation until he could no longer hold a shape in his mind, then leaned back from the table. He felt wonderfully calm, as though he'd crossed into some exalted plane of weariness. He arranged the tools and papers in the chest and slid it beneath the sideboard, then snuffed the lamp and tiptoed into the bedroom. Moonlight filtered through the curtains and illuminated the slope of his wife's shoulders beneath the quilt. How beautiful she was, his Milla; a pang of desire rose in Niklas's chest. He would tell her someday, he thought, and she would understand the glowing arcs in his mind, the rays of cool white light. She would not think him lazy or impractical. His Milla. Niklas eased into bed and laid his arm across his wife's shoulders, and in a few moments he was asleep.

Milla had grown to dislike Eva Prout during their first months in Iron Harbor. She disliked her pursed glances, full of disapproval; she disliked her voice, the archness that lifted the ends of her sentences, giving each question a mocking tone. Milla's English wasn't good enough to understand everything Eva Prout said, but she understood that Eva Prout thought she was young and a fool, and although Milla felt guilty for disliking Eva Prout, she was tired of being thought a fool. Besides Eva Prout, though, Milla did not know a single woman in Iron Harbor.

On the Monday after the accident Milla found herself in Eva Prout's parlor, sitting in a slat-backed rocker with a cup of tea and her heavy Bible balanced on her lap. Eva Prout was speaking about the man who'd been killed.

A good Christian, I hope, she said. I always recall Matthew: *Fear not them which kill the body, but are not able to kill the soul: but rather fear him which is able to destroy both soul and body in hell.* She cleared her throat. I pray for the poor lad's soul. So many wayward men in this town.

Milla nodded and thumbed her Bible open to the verse Eva had recited. *And a man's foes shall be they of his own household.* She traced her finger along the page. *He that loveth father or mother more than me is not worthy of me: and he that loveth son or daughter more than me is not worthy of me.* Milla looked up: Eva Prout was fixing her with a tight smile. Eva stood and excused herself to the kitchen, and returned with a plate holding a glistening ivory wedge of pear. Here, Eva said. Dear girl. With your tea.

Milla hesitated, then thanked Eva Prout and set the plate on her lap, resisting the urge to eat the entire wedge at once. Her gaze traveled up the oak mantel to a daguerreotype of a gaunt, somber man, Eva's father. He'd been a tin miner in Cornwall, and as Milla savored the pear's sweetness, she wondered if he'd been killed in a mine. She considered the question with numb clarity. She feared that one cold morning the steam whistle would sound, and suddenly she would be alone in this vast, godless country. Niklas had never spoken about his work, but she sensed in him a current of fear; this created in Milla's stomach a constant nervous flutter.

Often she found herself watching Niklas. She watched his

hands across the table as he spooned onion soup; she watched the slow play of his lips as he whispered evening prayers. He didn't pray often or with great fervor, and this troubled Milla, although his silence held a gravity that she thought must be near to prayer. He was the quietest and most gentle person she had ever known.

On their wedding night, in Niklas's father's house outside Oulu, Milla had hunched on the parlor floor and hugged herself against a chill that wouldn't stop. She was wearing her best linen dress and a borrowed beaver fur wrap. She was afraid to open the bedroom door, where Niklas was waiting. She began to cry. She loved the way his hair curled where it reached his brow; she loved the way he touched her cheek without speaking, as though he'd been rendered inarticulate by her beauty. But she feared what he would do when she entered the bedroom.

He tapped at the door. Milla. Open the door. I won't hurt you.

I know. I'm sorry.

She heard him rest his head against the door. Open the door. Please, Milla.

She knew little of men besides what she'd seen in her father: the sudden temper; the shockingly coarse hair on his hands; the tread of his boots, which had always struck in her heart a queer note of devotion and fear. She'd watched her mother expressionlessly mend her father's undergarments and knead his shoulders and pinch hard white nits from his head, and she wondered if her parents' indifference was a faded form of love. It disheartened Milla: her idea of love was so much closer to grace.

Milla, Niklas said. We don't have to do that. It's fine.

She knelt on the bedroom floor and crossed herself and murmured a rapid petition, for strength. She wiped the tears from
her swollen cheeks and opened the door. She couldn't look at
Niklas. He took her hand and led her into the room, then faced
the curtained window as she unfastened her dress and slid into
the cool, broad bed. Niklas extinguished the lamp and crawled in
beside her. How strange, she'd thought. In the darkness she
could not see his face, so she squeezed her eyes shut and imagined the smooth planes of his cheeks, his chin, his nose. How
strange, how strange, how strange. She turned and pulled him
toward her, gently at first, then with increasing strength.

You're nervous, Eva Prout said. She'd watched Milla slowly
eat the pear. You seem to have trouble on your mind.

Milla fidgeted in her chair then willed herself to stop.

I did wonder, Eva Prout said, if everything was right in your
house. I was ill last night, from those horrid potatoes at the mercantile, and I woke and noticed a lamp burning in your window.
Were you ill as well?

Milla shook her head.

Odd, Eva Prout said. I thought it odd to see a lamp burning
so late. Thought you must be ill.

The mantel clock ticked patiently. Milla said, Maybe you saw
the wrong window. Maybe next door.

No, no. She leaned toward Milla, grinning. I thought you
and your young husband must be quarreling.

Milla stood and murmured her apologies, that she must return home, and thanked Eva for the pear. Eva Prout took Milla's
teacup, smiling. Of course, she said. Dear girl. Of course.

Back in her cabin, Milla knelt beside the bed and prayed the penitential Psalms, then a petition to Saint Barbara, patron of miners. She prayed for strength against her temper and suspicions, and for Niklas's physical and spiritual health. But the prayers did not calm her as they usually did. She rose with the taste of stale tea in her mouth. She unscrewed the kitchen lamp's bulb: the oil was nearly gone. The sight unnerved her, but she shook it from her mind and refilled the lamp, then fetched the washbasin and began sorting the afternoon's laundry. Eva Prout, that angry woman, with her pears and oak mantel. She pulled Niklas's shirt from the basin, inhaling the thick odors of earth and sweat. An image formed in her mind of Niklas's ore-darkened face in the darkness of the mine. She wondered: Could you care for a person as much as you cared for your own soul? Could that *truly* be sin?

The announcement in the *Gazetteer* occupied a single square inch at the bottom of the second page: *Renowned Mathematician and Geometrician G. Craige to Address Young Men's Society in Halton.* Niklas sat in the dim change-house with the paper folded double. A dryness crept into his throat. *Famous Author of Over 100 Mathematical Proofs to Lecture on "Modern Analytical Geometrical Methods."* Niklas wove through the crowded room, then stopped, stuffed his hands in his pockets, and sat on a bench near the door. He reread the announcement until the steam whistle sounded. Then he folded the newspaper carefully and placed it inside his shirt, and started toward the mine shaft's massive oak bracing.

That night, as he knelt with Milla in their bedroom, his mind strayed toward circles and ellipses, the austere perfection of conic sections. *Construct a square, equal in area to a given circle.*

His wife's voice was steady as a metronome. *For thine is the kingdom, and the power, and the glory, for ever. Amen.* Niklas crawled beneath the heavy quilt. He was too anxious for sleep, and Milla must have sensed this: she turned to him and grasped the hem of his nightshirt.

Later he sat before a smudged diagram, the tip of his ruler pressed against his chin. Beside the diagram a column of notation spilled halfway down the page. How to proceed? The way was as dark as an unlit mine shaft. He sank the compass into a clean sheet of paper and twirled a sleek arc. He remembered as a boy sitting beneath a weeping willow near his father's house, watching fireflies carve parabolas into the dusky night. The curves had remained lit up in his mind for hours, and sometimes even now he saw forms as if they'd been etched by a brilliant light. The curves glowed in his mind.

He struck an arc, then opened the compass and struck a second arc and labeled the intersections α and β. He took up the ruler and transected the first arc, extending his line to the edge of the page, then carved a large, slow circle. Yes. He ruled another line, then another. On a second page he began describing the angles and line segments, one equation following the other like freight cars behind a locomotive. He felt euphoric, full of light. His hand began to cramp, but he didn't stop writing.

Near dawn, eye-weary from the guttering lamplight, Niklas drew three dark lines beneath a lone equation. His heart was pounding so intensely that he wondered if Milla could hear it in her sleep. He rolled the papers together and placed them in the chest, then slid the chest beneath the sideboard. He extinguished the lamp and opened the bedroom door and slipped into bed beside his wife. Milla shuddered, then relaxed. Niklas had a sudden, ecstatic urge to wake her and show her the papers, to explain what they meant—but no, not yet. He kissed Milla's shoulder and closed his eyes, inhaling her rich scent. The image of his wife's face glowed in his mind, as if traced by fireflies.

Milla had run out of matches and could not light the stove the next morning. The fire had died during the night, and she woke in a frigid cabin to find the tin matchbox empty. Niklas said nothing, stuffed three pork biscuits into his pocket, and stepped out into the gray morning. Milla wrapped herself in a woolen shawl and laced her cornette under her chin. She did not want to wait for the mercantile to open, and she did not want to borrow matches from Eva Prout. She did not want to borrow anything from Eva Prout.

She vaguely remembered a box of phosphorous matches in the chest beneath the sideboard, so she dragged the chest into the middle of the floor. Locked. She didn't have the key; Niklas was surely carrying it, for safekeeping. Milla felt a swell of pride in her husband's prudence, but beneath that a prickle of annoyance. She rattled the lock, then rummaged in Niklas's steamer trunk and fetched a hammer and thin nail. She buttoned her shawl and stepped out into the eye-watering chill, then held the nail against the boot stone while she rapped it with the hammer. Her breath ribboned out in pale clouds. She battered the nail into a rough L, then stepped inside and worked the nail into the lock, eyes closed, probing for the single tumbler, until finally the lock gave with a sharp click.

In the chest there was a tin of matches and a sheaf of papers, pens, a small book, some brass tools. She removed the tools and book and placed them on the table. She fanned the papers, and a queer sense of dread crept over her. It was Niklas's penmanship. Crosses lay broken and skewed, surrounded by circles and split by sharp arcs. Dark, ornate symbols covered the pages. There were letters, but the letters spelled no words, and the thought entered Milla's mind that the pages were meant for another woman, a secret code—but that was impossible, it must be impossible.

She leafed through the papers, her heart fluttering like a trapped bird. She'd heard rumors of foreign men who wrote in strange scripts and spoke in tongues, whose lives were full of deceit and carnality—and Eva Prout's warning, of the godless men in Iron Harbor. She stuffed the papers into the chest and paced to the far side of the kitchen. A bitter, metallic taste rose in her mouth, and for a moment Milla thought she might be sick. She spat onto the floor. Her mind was full of noise, and she crossed herself and recited the Lord's Prayer, but the words seemed to vanish in the cold air.

She slumped into a chair and imagined Niklas's calm, curious gaze melting into a vacant stare, a stranger's stare. She thought: his soul. She rushed to the bedroom, and just as she reached the chamber set her stomach heaved, a series of deep, choking coughs. Please, she thought, please, please, please. She swallowed a cup of water, then sat on the kitchen floor with her Bible opened to John: the great crusader, the martyr in a hostile land. *Behold,* she read, *the hour cometh, yea, is now come, that ye shall be scattered, every man to his own, and shall leave me alone: and yet I am not alone, because the Father is with me.* Her finger trembled against the page. *In the world ye shall have tribulation, but be of good cheer; I have overcome the world.*

The words did not calm her. She must save him, she thought—she must save herself. She opened the stove door and from the woodbox fetched birch twigs and a chunk of pine, then struck a match and watched flames crawl over the dry wood. She gathered the papers into a bundle and tied them with string, then placed the bundle atop the crackling fire. Pages peeled away, flames painting the symbols brown then a sudden, brilliant orange. Milla knelt before the stove, her lips pursed as if against a driving wind, and watched the fire burn.

That evening Niklas hurried down the long, sloping road to town, and as he passed the lit-up windows of the mercantile, he stopped. He peered in at the brimming barrels of sugar and dried beans and saleratus. He stepped inside; Henry Johnson nodded at him, his hands clasped over a smudged white apron. Niklas pointed at a barrel of small green peaches.

Peaches, Henry Johnson said. Niklas nodded.

Johnson took four peaches from the barrel, glancing back at Niklas after each one, until Niklas said, Enough. Niklas paid thirty cents for the peaches, pausing for a moment at the cost, then placed them in his coat pocket and smiled at Henry Johnson. Johnson nodded again.

That night he devoured his fried pork and cabbage and waited impatiently as Milla cleaned the dishes. When she'd finished, he reached into his coat pocket, then held his clenched fists behind his back. He smiled at Milla. A surprise, he said. Guess.

She looked up from the table, expressionless.

Guess, Niklas said. Please.

Milla rose and stood before Niklas, eyes downcast. She shook her head.

Niklas brought his fists from behind his back. Peaches, he said. Last of the season. Milla smiled, still not looking at him, and set the peaches on the kitchen table. She kissed Niklas's cheek, then turned and walked slowly into the bedroom, closing the door behind her.

Niklas stared after her—was she unhappy? Perhaps the cost, or the smallness of the fruit... He shook his head. He took a bowl from the sideboard and placed the peaches inside, then snuffed the kitchen lamp.

In the bedroom he pulled on his nightshirt and crawled into bed, the frame groaning against his weight. His muscles were sore from sorting rock, but Niklas felt as though he could work until dawn: tomorrow Craige would be in Halton; he had one night to complete his proof. Milla turned to him, her small fist pressed against his chest. She buried her head against his shoulder, and her entire body shuddered.

What? Niklas asked.

Silence.

What is it?

Milla lay very still. Niklas felt detached, his body a limp useless trunk but his mind so restless and vast. He would finish the proof tonight. Niklas stroked Milla's neck, soothing her toward sleep, and finally her fist relaxed. He waited until her breathing had deepened into long, distant sighs, then slipped from beneath the quilt.

The puncheon floor was cold beneath his feet. He padded into the kitchen and closed the door, then knelt and slid the chest from beneath the sideboard. He set the chest on the kitchen table and from around his neck removed the key. With a snap the lock opened.

Gone. A shiver raced over Niklas's skin. He removed the text-book, compass, ruler, ink, blotting paper, and pens, then turned the chest upside down and watched crumbled bits of paper flutter like moths in the dim lamplight. Gone.

He paced quickly around the kitchen, then took up the chest and ran his fingers along the empty inside. He crouched on the floor and hugged his knees to his chest and bowed his head. Milla had found his papers—what did she think of him now, her husband? A thick sob rose in Niklas's throat. And what of his proof? He could reconstruct part of it—perhaps Craige could examine the fragments, perhaps he would see potential. . . . He heard a rustle of bedsheets as his wife shifted in her sleep. And what of Milla?

He sat motionless on the floor for a long time, then dragged himself to his feet and took a wrinkled newspaper from his coat pocket. He would show Craige. He took up a pen and ruled a heavy black line atop news of ore assays and shaft depths and ship tonnage. He would steer him through the subtle currents of the proof. And when Craige had recognized his struggle as something notable—something extraordinary, even—he would explain it to Milla. He would introduce her to his problem, as a depraved man might introduce his wife to his lover.

They woke together the next morning. Milla shuffled to the kitchen to raise the fire and heat yesterday's biscuits for break-fast, and Niklas slumped on the bed, his arms and legs feeling as though they were submerged in syrup. He'd slept less than an hour. In his coat pocket was a scrawled but finished version of the proof. *Construct a square*, he found himself thinking, *equal in area to a given circle*. The thought made him queasy, like the smell of whiskey after a daylong drunk.

He dressed in the chilly bedroom and drank a cup of tea, and as his mind cleared he felt a stir of excitement. Craige was here, in this state. On this godforsaken peninsula. He kissed Milla, his stubbled skin rough against her smooth cheek.

I'll be late tonight, he said. Prout wants to raise the main brace on a new shaft. Says it's going to pay fifty cents overtime.

Milla nodded, her head lowered against her chest.

Hey, he said, are you feeling right? He laid a finger beneath her chin and raised it; her eyes shone bright with tears. Don't do that. Please.

I'm fine, she said, blotting her tears with the back of her hand. I'm having woman troubles, is all.

Niklas nodded. Rest today, he said. I'll bring something from the mercantile. He kissed her again and pulled on his coat, then stepped out into the dim morning.

He walked to the mine site, but instead of going to the change-house, he stopped at the captain's office. Prout was sitting at his desk touching a match to his pipe. What? he said.

Niklas curled his lips, clutching the right side of his stomach. Sick.

Prout drew a dense puff of smoke. You're sick you don't get paid. What's wrong with you?

Niklas stared blankly at Prout.

What's wrong? Prout shouted. He sighed. Work tomorrow. He pointed at the ground. Tomorrow morning. Work.

Yes, Niklas said, tomorrow. Thank you. He winced, and hobbled from the office.

Fifteen minutes later he stood at Iron Harbor's depot, a

raised plank platform between the temperance hall and barber-shop. The morning train would arrive soon; he would reach Halton by noon. Later he could catch the evening train and be home before nine. He stamped his feet against the cold and stared down the curving tracks, a pang in his stomach reminding him that he hadn't eaten breakfast. He pulled a cold flour biscuit from his pocket and chewed it slowly. Finally he saw a thread of smoke in the distance, then beneath it a tiny black locomotive. He touched his breast pocket, where the proof was folded, and waited for the train to rattle to a stop.

In Halton, Niklas went to the first boardinghouse he saw and paid two cents to use the bathtub. He stripped off his clothes and from his lunch bucket removed a clean shirt and a pair of balled-up trousers. His boots were caked with dirt, but although he rubbed them until the washcloth was blood-colored, the boots didn't gain any shine. He worked for a few minutes, then gave up. A comb was chained to a brass ring in the wall, and he slicked his hair against his skull, then scrutinized his reflection in the cloudy mirror. Then he stuffed his soiled clothes into his lunch bucket and reemerged in Halton's downtown.

A breeze sliced in from the lake and froze Niklas's hair against his neck, and he shivered, wishing he had an overcoat. It was past noon, but he was too nervous to eat, so he walked to the library where the Young Men's Society was to meet. He paused with his hand on the wrought-iron railing. The library was a tall brick building with a portico and fluted columns, and Niklas let his gaze travel up a column to the capital: arcs and whorls were carved in the stone, the large whorls curling into smaller ones, the smallest ones curling into nothing. The sight of such unexpected beauty lifted Niklas's heart; he took a deep breath and climbed the low steps, and pulled open the door.

Inside, the library was warm and smelled richly of cedar; there was a crimson carpet and a pair of high bookshelves filled with volumes. He saw an open door, and through it a row of chairs, and then he noticed a handbill announcing Craige's lecture. Niklas slipped into the empty room. He was nearly three hours early and exhausted, and hungry, but he took a seat in the chair nearest the podium and set his lunch bucket between his feet. He would wait.

She had sat at the kitchen table after he'd left, sipping tea and staring at his empty cup. The stove had pushed the chill from the room, and she took off her shawl and busied herself stripping the bedsheets and drawing a tub of water for wash. She set the kettle on, and as she waited for it to warm, she knelt beside the kitchen table and prayed. But even as her lips moved, she found herself thinking about Niklas's papers, and those strange symbols.

She believed he was needed at the mine, yet at the same time she allowed herself a sliver of disbelief. She did not want to be made a fool. She supposed she was as foolish as any woman, but she did not want the entire town to think her a fool; she did not want Eva Prout to think her a fool. She rose and stood in the middle of the small room, surveying the coarse pine walls, the pitted table, the bowl of hard green peaches. Then she took the kettle off the stove and tied her cloak at the neck, and stepped out into the cold morning.

The sky was low and gray-white, the color of wood ash; it had snowed the night before, and the streets of Iron Harbor looked as though they were dusted with flour. Milla walked past the schoolhouse and Methodist church, and at the mercantile bought a pound of buckwheat and some dried pea beans. Henry Johnson weighed her purchases on the scale then silently tallied the bill. She paid and stepped outside, gathering her cloak against the wind, and then she saw her husband.

She froze. Niklas was leaning against the temperance house, on the far side of the street, gazing down the railroad tracks toward Algoma. Milla stepped quickly back against the mercantile. He was wearing mine clothes but was waiting for the train, headed—where?—to Johns Corner or Halton or as far as Marquette. He began pacing in a small circle, head bowed, and Milla sensed in him a restlessness that started a tremble in her stomach. She recalled his smile the night before, when he'd stood with his hands behind his back. *Guess*, he'd said. *A surprise.* Those peaches: what had they meant? What had his smile meant?

Just then she heard the faint airy whistle of the locomotive. She watched the train lurch to a halt, then saw Niklas hurry to the first car and step inside. It was a cargo train mainly, with two small passenger cars and no ladies' car. Fine: she would sit with the men. Milla rushed across the street, head low, and opened the second car's door and sat on a hard oak bench. When she craned her neck, she could glimpse Niklas's blond curls through the door's glass panel.

At Johns Corner the train rattled to a halt, but Niklas didn't move; a half-dozen passengers disembarked, and a portly man wearing muttonchop sideburns climbed aboard and sat beside Milla. He smelled powerfully, of tobacco and sour sweat. He regarded her silently. Milla sat with her eyes closed, reciting ten Apostles' Creeds, using her knuckles as counting beads. The train shuddered over the iron straps. At Halton she rushed to the side of the car and peered out the window, and saw Niklas step down onto the platform and begin walking quickly toward the center of town.

She followed him across the street and watched him disappear into a whitewashed boardinghouse. A wave of cold nausea rushed through her. She thought: He does not love me. She thought: He has never loved me. Milla stared at the closed boardinghouse door, willing herself to stand erect, not to falter. She thought: I am alone, and this notion struck her with the force of a slap.

There were no stages back to Iron Harbor and no train until evening. She stood on the sidewalk, ignoring the stares of passersby, and was about to begin the long walk home when she saw Niklas emerge from the boardinghouse in clean clothes, his hair combed. He'd been inside only fifteen minutes. Milla hesitated, her body tensed as if ready to sprint, then started after him.

He stopped outside the lending library and stared up at the stone pediment, then climbed the low steps and went inside. A library, Milla thought, her mind refusing to uncloud. My husband is going to a library. She counted to twenty. When he hadn't appeared, she counted to a hundred. Then she climbed the steps and pulled open the heavy door, and stepped inside.

There was an open door, and through it Milla saw her husband as if she were seeing a stranger: a handsome young man sitting in a library, in his Sunday clothes, alone, waiting. A sudden image flashed in her mind: her forgotten parcel, eleven cents' worth of buckwheat and dried pea beans, on the train seat headed to Marquette. Milla untied her cornette and sat at the reading table. She told herself to be patient, to wait and see— she hadn't lost him. Not yet. So far all she'd lost was eleven cents.

Later, after the door had been closed for a long time, men in waistcoats and boiled shirts and thin leather boots began filing out, a few in deep discussion but most wearing dull expressions. Milla rose, and when her husband did not appear, she moved to the door: he was standing near the podium, gesturing to a tall, stooped man with a trim beard and spectacles. They were looking at a paper Niklas was holding, and Niklas was pointing at different parts of the page. Look here, he seemed to be saying. And here. And here.

She had never seen him so agitated. His voice held a slight tremor, and even from across the room she could see a sheen of perspiration on his forehead. Behind the podium, symbols were printed on a large slate—those strange symbols, but above them were the words *Young Men's Society* and *Modern Analytical Geometrical Methods*. Young Men's Society: the words caused in Milla a twinge of confusion and relief. She unconsciously took a step toward Niklas. The tall man was leaning away from her husband, as if cowed by the force of his words, and Niklas pointed again at the paper, then looked at the man and fell silent.

The bespectacled man raised a finger. *Wait.* He pointed at the page and said nothing for a moment. Then he removed his spectacles, wiping his face with one hand, and began speaking, pausing to draw invisible lines in the air. Niklas watched his lips, nodding. The tall man laid his hand on Niklas's arm and smiled genially. He shook his head, as if in consolation. Niklas stared at him and mouthed the words, Yes. I understand. Thank you. The tall man turned and began gathering papers from the podium.

She watched her husband until the tall man had departed and Niklas was the last person in the room. He stood alone beside the podium, shoulders slumped, head bowed to his chest. How could she ever know him? Milla felt her heart welling with hope and despair—an astonishing, unbearable fullness—and she moved toward her husband, and saw in an instant the grace of his bent arms, his neck, the line of his chin. A perfect form, eternal, as if chiseled from stone.

CHILDREN OF HUNGER

Sault Ste. Marie, 1822

SHE remembers the heat, that night, and the smell of gunsmoke drifting over the straits. Bonfires flickered along the riverbank, throwing shadows from dancing *voyageurs*; occasionally a métis woman stepped into the firelight and imitated their clumsy reel. Traders and natives sat in loose circles, waving at mosquitoes that hung as thick as fog. Shrill strains from a fiddle rose and faded in the chalky sky.

In their cabin, beside the Presbyterian church: a groan, a slap of damp flesh, a finger of moonlight pointing at her white-blond hair on the pillow. Her husband's eyes were squeezed shut in concentration, and Julia found herself staring at his eyelids, the skin wrinkled and slack, like tiny silk draperies. The sight was mesmerizing and strangely arousing. She twisted his nightshirt in her fist.

Then a rap on the door that immediately repeated itself: *Docteur, s'il vous plaît! À l'aide!*

She crossed her ankles behind his back. Finish, she said.

Let me up.

William. Please.

Docteur Barber! Frypans rattled on their hooks against the kitchen wall.

He pried her ankles apart and staggered to his feet. *Un moment!* he called, then to Julia said, Stupid girl. He fumbled with his trousers. These moments, they're important. Can you understand that?

She wiped her furrowed brow. Most likely a half-breed with a bellyache.

William stamped into his boots. You act like a child, then complain when I treat you like one. You should be praying that no one's sick, instead of thinking about yourself.

Please, dear, Julia said. It's not such an awful request, is it? To stay in bed with your wife?

He snorted, and snatched his pigskin bag.

But he paused at the door, his neck gleaming with sweat, a thatch of hair smeared against his forehead. He was a bear of a man, ponderous and irritable, with a queer fussiness about his work: Julia was forbidden to disturb him while he wrote in his medical journal, forbidden to dust his leather-bound textbooks. They stood on a shelf beside the bed, giving the room a faint musty smell. She told herself she admired his dedication, though in truth it troubled her; some evenings he devoured dinner with his head bowed, then changed into his nightshirt without speaking, and she wondered if he even noticed her. But his journal was dotted with strange, elliptical poems, about the two of them together on a stormy shore, so Julia watched him, hoping.

He stepped through the door without saying a word.

Detroit, 1860

Dr. Pearse insists he's been thinking about Julia for several years. He sits beside her on the settee in her parlor, a hint of bitter coffee on his breath. He is forty, she supposes, but wears his beard in a youthful Imperial and speaks with brash confidence. She prefers him to Dr. Jacobsen and Dr. Lee; both of them declined her invitation to dinner tonight.

"It's generous of you to escort an old woman," Julia says. "These evenings can be so boring: a room full of drunk physicians, boasting about the past."

"I'm honored," Dr. Pearse says. "Every important doctor in the city will be there—and of course, you're far from old. A young girl would be lucky to have your healthy flush." His gaze skips down her yellow crinoline.

She is still somewhat beautiful, she thinks: her hair has grayed, but lost none of its thick gloss. How many of her husband's colleagues stared at her that way, with the same pleased curiosity? Broussard, and McAdam, Lowell. Gipson, the beautiful boy. Though they were different: their desire was rooted in envy, of William's work.

"I was a student of his," the doctor says. "He was a remarkable man, all of us sensed it. I remember one morning he arrived at the college without his lecture—he'd forgotten it at home, I believe—so he proceeded to speak about the digestive system from memory, for two hours. I still carry his text."

He reaches inside his jacket with a bashful grin, and produces a maroon book, scuffed flat at the heel and spine. *Experiments and Observations on Hunger and the Physiology of Digestion,* by *William Barber, M.D.* Julia turns it over in her hands.

She has never read the book, a fact she savors guiltily. Much of it, she knows, was drawn from his medical journals, which he wrote in every night while Julia lay in bed. Every morning, after he'd eaten a silent breakfast and departed for the garrison hospital, Julia removed the journal from his desk drawer and read the most recent entry as she sipped tea.

The doctor continues: "I ate dinner with him, four years ago at Professor Benson's house. He spoke about you—that was when I first wondered who you were."

She nods, to mask her surprise. "May I ask what he said?"

"He told me you were critical to his work. I remember clearly: he said, 'Before purchasing a single instrument, every young doctor should first win the hand of an agreeable wife, as I did. It will be the richest investment of your career.' "

She feels a surge of anger, which slowly fades to melancholy. *An investment:* she supposes it's a true enough description. What had William given her, in exchange for his career? Countless hours of uncertain waiting, enough time to map every narrow path to happiness, then watch them fade into regret. Though she'd gained a son, Jacob; perhaps, then, the arrangement wasn't so unfair.

"You're very kind," she says. "Now, if you wouldn't mind, I'd like to leave. My son will be at dinner. I want to be there when he arrives."

Dr. Pearse rises awkwardly. "Of course. I'll call for the carriage."

His hand brushes Julia's as he takes the book. She watches him cross the room, her fingers warm with the memory of his touch. She waits until the front door slams, then climbs the stairs and unlocks the door to William's library. Orange light seeps through the shuttered window; the air smells of mildew and stale pipe smoke. His medical journals lean in a row on the bookshelf, the leather bindings covered with wrinkles as faint and precise as fingerprints. As she scans the chilly room, her mind fills with an image from her wedding night: William standing shirtless before an open window, listening to his own heartbeat through an India rubber stethoscope, while she lay beneath a white sheet, watching him, her body aching. What a wonder, she thinks, how earnest I was, how much I hoped, how hard I fought myself. Yet here I am, now, this very evening. The world is not so terrible as the ministers claim.

Julia locks the door and hurries downstairs, then steps out to the waiting carriage.

They laid the injured boy on a cot in the cabin's sickroom, where he drifted in a fever for four days, mumbling vague phrases, his lips curled in pain. Twice he woke Julia with shouts, for his *maman*. The fifth morning, she peered through the open sickroom door while her husband inspected the boy's wound. William swabbed with a cloth until it came away streaked with blood. The boy's breathing sharpened to a gasp.

She shut the door, then gathered breakfast dishes from the table. The cabin was small, just a storeroom and smoky kitchen, a small bedroom and sickroom huddled around a stone fire-place. There was no parlor, so the kitchen mantel held Julia's few treasures: a stunted, lacquered tree in a ceramic jar; a stuffed bluebird perched on a twig, head cocked; a tiny snuff-box, filigreed with a trumpeting angel. She'd brought the objects from Detroit, to display for visitors—but there were no visitors at the garrison, just soldiers and *voyageurs* and black-haired natives sleeping in lodges along the riverbank. Julia knew every knot and splinter in the cabin's wooden walls.

She set a pot of water on, then scraped the dishes clean. Dishes to wash, then William's gloves to mend, then the bedroom floor to scour with sand. Ordinarily the list filled her with gloom, but that morning she'd awakened with a taste of bile in her throat; the sensation had caused her to stiffen with excitement.

She set the dishes in a stack, and from William's desk took a pen and sheet of paper.

August 10, 1822

Dearest most wonderful Sister Susan,

This morning I woke all aflutter, as though a family of squirrels had nested in my belly. Tell me how you felt when Henry was inside you. Please send news! You promised last month to write daily but I've received only four letters since. Cruel sister! You know I'm well enough talking to myself, but I'd much rather read your letters.

There is a boy with us, one of the Canadian paddlers, who was shot in the stomach but refuses to die. William is all in a feeze caring for him. His appearance reminds me of Deborah Grant's cousin—the taller one, the bully? Do you remember how

William emerged from the sickroom and tossed a blood-stained cloth onto the table. He took up his jacket from a peg beside the door.

I heard a noise, Julia said. Is he awake?

I left him a bell, he said. Bring him white food if he rings. Bread, potatoes, milk, cheese. Understand?

White food.

William patted his trouser pocket, frowning. I have not a single clean handkerchief.

Julia watched him fasten the jacket's buttons over his stomach. A reddish-black smear of blood marked his wrist. She said, I'll wash some tomorrow.

He glanced at her; then his gaze flicked to the unfinished letter. Send my greetings to your sister and Edward. Ask her to send your magazines—you must be tired of the old issues.

Julia thought for a moment to mention her sickness, then struck the idea from her mind. He'd accuse me of nervousness, she thought, send me to bed with a dose of jalap. Better to wait until I'm certain, then watch his face fall slack with joy.

I will, she said. And I'll ask her to forward your surgery journals, if they've arrived.

William smiled absently, then tugged open the door. Julia hurried to the bedroom window and watched him tramp down the sloping path to the hospital, head bowed in thought. Beyond him she could see a sliver of the glimmering straits, and farther north the vast, shadowy forest. She watched until he'd passed behind the barracks.

She'd sensed William's stiffness even during their initial meetings, but his letters had pleased her: *Tonight as I walked home I did not bother to look up at the stars,* he'd written, *so humbled are they by your eyes.* She'd reasoned that since he was capable of small acts of tenderness, he must surely be capable of large ones. The first evening they met, at the medical society ball in Detroit, she'd told him she thought doctors were indeed angels, but fallen angels: bringers of pain and sorrow, their mere sight a cause of distress. He'd smiled uneasily. *And how do you interpret my mere sight?* She'd laughed but did not reply. She was twenty-one years old, fourteen years his junior, but felt marvelously confident. They'd sat in straight-backed chairs at the edge of the ballroom, watching couples whirl across the creaking floor. She'd waited for William to request a dance, but instead he'd abruptly stood, and disappeared through the wide double doors.

Now she opened his desk drawer and withdrew the heavy journal. She opened it to his previous night's entry.

August 9, 1822

This evening the boy's fever broke and the wound's foetid odor diminished. Bled fifteen ounces to relieve arterial excitement, and lanced an abscess to reveal three pea-sized pebbles of swan shot. Sloughing of the integument has commenced; the wound resembles nothing so much as a chapped, puckered mouth. In morning light, after he has taken breakfast, I can glimpse into the stomach, which is as roiling and turbulent as the straits outside.

The boy's condition is marvelous: I have a clear view of the inner workings of his digestive system. Neither Dunglison nor Magendie, in their most fitful dreams, could have conceived of such a circumstance.

Must write Hornbeck, to relate the news.

> *In wind that whipped the whitening sea,*
> *I stood atop a rocky mount,*
> *beneath the eyes of God, alone, my pleas*
> *consumed by the firmament.*

A bell tinkled. She closed the journal, momentarily piqued at her absence from William's poem, then opened the sickroom door.

The boy was awake, his eyes free of feverish weight. A blanket was strewn across his lap; his bare arms and legs hung over the sides of the small cot. A mottled gray bandage was bound about his midsection.

Good morning, she said. How do you feel?

The boy stared at her. Like a dead man.

His cheeks were fleshy and pale, covered by a wispy orange beard, and his slack mouth revealed two missing front teeth. Corded muscle sloped from his neck to his freckled shoulders. He was seventeen, or perhaps eighteen—neither boy nor man, but a thwarted ambition toward one or the other. His name was Guillaume Roleau.

Would you like a cup of water?

Rum. He spat weakly through his missing teeth. Or brandy. And some meat.

We don't have rum, she said. I can bring you milk and bread.

You may as well shoot me again. He attempted a laugh, but the result was a desperate cough. Julia turned toward the kitchen.

Wait. He raised two fingers. I want to see it.

She hesitated. Where was William? At the hospital treating consumptive soldiers, or hunting for roots in the swampy forest. Or pacing along the garrison walls, hands clasped behind his back, at once a hundred yards and a thousand miles from their cabin.

Julia drew a stool beside the cot. She unspooled the boy's bandage, then picked at the crusted square of lint.

Bon sang, the boy hissed. It hurts.

She fetched a pitcher and dribbled water into the lint, until it trickled down his chest. Bluish veins crisscrossed the boy's white abdomen. She peeled back the fabric. A raw, glistening wound gaped below his breast, the surrounding skin frayed and black, as though it had been scorched. Inside the wound, a rib curved above the reddish tip of his lung. As Julia watched, the lung crumpled, then swelled.

There had been an accident, according to her husband's journal. The shot had forced wadding and swan load deep into the boy's chest, the muzzle's flash setting his shirt on fire. William's entry from that night was brief and precise: *Cleaned the wound of extraneous material, then applied a carbonated fermenting poultice and muriate of ammonia. As I probed, a gruel-colored wash of partially digested food oozed from the perforation in his stomach and spilled onto the floor. He will surely die before morning.*

Cover it, the boy gasped.

She placed clean lint over the bloody tissue. The wound's sourness mingled with the boy's oniony odor.

He laid his right hand across his abdomen. When will I be strong enough to paddle?

I don't know. I'm very sorry.

He stared at the dirty bandage in her hands. He said, Tell me your name.

Julia.

Julia, he repeated. I've seen you in my dreams, these nights. You are surely an angel.

The carriage clatters down Jefferson Avenue, past the Negro church and poorhouse, the empty fish market. "I was saddened to hear of his passing," Dr. Pearse says. "Such a loss—not just to his loved ones, but to the city. The profession."

Julia nods but says nothing: a practiced, dignified silence. A fire bell clangs in the distance, despite the drizzling rain.

"Was he very sick, when he died?" Dr. Pearse leans across the narrow seat. "If you don't mind—sharing such personal details. His death was sudden, from what I heard."

"He was sick for a long time."

Dr. Pearse nods expectantly, but Julia looks away. Dusk has settled in a vague mist over the city; on the sidewalk she sees a lamplighter standing atop a ladder, his arms bathed in the gas lamp's white glow. A gaunt man, no sturdier than a boy—as William was, when he died.

She remembers, after the funeral, climbing the stairs to William's study with her son, Jacob. She neatened stray journals, searching for William's tattered black address book. Behind the desk, in a cedar box, she found four bundles of paper tied with silk surgeon's thread. Julia sat in his chair, sifting through brittle pages; it seemed that William had saved copies of every letter he'd sent, to every professor and publisher and country doctor. At the bottom of the box she found a sheaf of neatly penned notecards, covered with her own fluid script. She took one up and read it aloud.

October 22, 1819

Sweetest most sadly distant William,

Winter is upon us. Swans, brants, and cranes have flown south, the naked oaks and maples offering chilly waves of farewell. The birds' desire for comfort must be what leads them, as it leads us all, though animals act on pure instinct, whereas we must temper our desires with propriety. Would you agree with me that this is a shame?

Your dearly devoted,
Julia

Julia chuckled, giving rise to a thick sob. She picked up another.

July 9, 1820

My dearest Julia,

I've made arrangements for our travel. We will depart on the steamer Walk-in-the-water *on August 7 at 6:15 A.M. and arrive at the garrison the following evening. I trust you will bring the necessary plates, kettles, sheeting, curtains, etc. to make ours a comfortable home.*

My dear, my own. How can I be content until then, without you? My heart leaps to the memory of your voice. My blood rushes to the sound of your footsteps.

Your devoted,
William

She remembers the note with a mixture of bitterness and wonder, and grief. William had possessed warmth, but only in gestures and glances, brief lines in letters. How was it possible, Julia wonders now, that she'd convinced herself to love his sternness? And yet she'd loved his fierce stare, the way his eyebrows arched together to form a curve; it eased the tightness in her heart. She'd told herself she was young and impulsive, and he was prudent and deeply mature, and that together they made a balance—as though impulsiveness and youth needed to be balanced. As though joy could balance sorrow and produce calm.

"Difficult to believe it's been thirty-five years since the book's publication." Dr. Pearse shakes his head, staring out the rain-streaked window. "I was just a boy. Not even in long trousers."

Perhaps she was too selfish? William's work, after all, had given her visits to Paris and Hamburg, a pink pearl necklace and ivory brooch, a beautiful coupé with morocco trim. And a son: she tries to imagine her life without Jacob, but the thought dissolves in an unpleasant haze. She smiles at Dr. Pearse.

"You'll be celebrated tonight, of course," he says. "You're the only witness to his famous experiments. Besides the *voyageur,* of course."

"I wasn't a witness."

Dr. Pearse nods cautiously.

"It was William and the boy, alone in the sickroom." Julia shrugs: a vague, helpless gesture. "I can hardly recall those days."

September brought cold morning breezes off the straits, and the disappearance of a fever that all summer had shaken Julia with chills. After breakfast she walked to the sutler's and bought flour or eggs or a few yards of cloth, then strolled along the grassy riverbank, watching *voyageurs* load canoes in thin cotton shirts and breechclouts, moccasins and knee-high leggings. She shivered in her cloak, the heavy wool seeming to burden her with gloom. Opposite the straits, she could see the roof of their cabin, a thread of smoke winding from the chimney, and her mood lifted at the sight; then her thoughts settled on William.

He'd been cheerier, since the boy's arrival, but no less remote: he woke at dawn and raised the fire, then examined the boy before leaving for the hospital. At dusk he returned and drank a cup of tea, then disappeared into the sickroom. Julia sat at the kitchen table, an unfinished letter before her. The only sound in the cabin was the faint scratch of her pen.

One night William emerged from the sickroom and hurried to the bookshelf; Julia listened to the crisp riffle of pages, then a long silence. Finally he stood at the table, hands thrust in his vest.

Is the boy well?

He frowned, jingling coins in his pocket. He goes without food, and becomes hungry. He eats, and his hunger disappears. Why do you suppose that is?

Julia smiled cautiously.

Come on, William said.

Wind rushed against the cabin door, the sound like a chorus of whispers. Julia shook her head. I don't know.

Of course you don't. He grinned, and smoothed her hair against her neck. No one knows, my dear.

She grabbed William's hand, but he smiled uneasily and peeled her fingers from his wrist. We'll try later, he said. Tonight—I promise.

She woke the next morning with a gnarled cramp in her abdomen. She set the kettle on, then walked a dozen slow turns around the kitchen. *I've failed again,* she thought, and tried to force her mind toward a pleasant thought: the mail boat's arrival, a likely letter from Susan. Last night, she'd failed once again to rouse William; Julia thought bitterly that his vigor was probably drained by his constant work. *I've failed, I've failed, I've failed again*. She hummed the words as a grim marching song.

She began sweeping the kitchen, then slammed the broom to the floorboards. She hated the frustrating hesitations in William's conversation, the agonizing uncertainty before every touch. Julia often imagined them as stiff, white-haired strangers, sitting across from each other at breakfast without speaking, and the thought inevitably left her angry and sad. A child would relieve their troubles: William's distance, her own loneliness. The cabin seemed filled with her own stale breath.

She swept the hearth, as the boy paced in the sickroom. She stopped sweeping, and the pacing stopped; then the bell rang.

She leaned into the sickroom. Good morning, Monsieur Roleau.

Bonjour Madame. Have you brought this snow?

Julia smiled politely. Would you like a cup of tea?

I remember a story about a woman with white hair, a snow-woman—a bringer of snow, with a shake of her head. She would fly across the sky in a gold *traineau* drawn by elk, and shake her white hair, and leave snowstorms in her path. Could this be you?

She smiled again. The boy was only three years her junior but possessed a child's delight in simple jokes. Yet he was not a simpleton: some afternoons she heard him circling the room, but during William's examination he claimed to be too pained to raise an arm. He could not read, but seemed to know a thousand paddling songs, which he sang in a coarse but melodious voice.

I'll bring your tea, she said.

Talk with me, please. For a few minutes.

Julia stepped into the kitchen, followed by the boy's groan.

She'd tended ill patients before, but never for longer than three days; the boy had been in the sickroom for five weeks. On Saturday mornings William changed the boy's bandage, while she listened at the door: the boy's tone was sullen and curt, but William seemed calmly pleased. This caused a pang of jealousy in Julia.

She fetched the tea tin and cup, then poured on steaming water, humming a mindless, lilting tune. With a start she realized she was humming one of the boy's paddling songs.

You remind me of a Chippewa woman I knew, he said, when Julia returned. No—don't be offended.

She offered him the teacup, then stood at the open door.

She was married, but that means nothing in their tribes. The women are allowed to go with other men, do you understand? We camped near their village on Lac du Bois Blanc, waiting for a storm to die, and she would come to our camp and sit at the fire. She was very sad, like you, with a sad smile. She was like— He squinted, licking his lips. She was like a tree, full of ripe fruit. Do you understand?

Mind yourself, Julia said. Please.

When we loaded the canoes, she pulled at my sleeve until it tore. She said I looked like her husband, who had been captured by Sioux. Her name was Woman of the Green Valley. Or something like that, green woman, woman of something green.

You left her there, of course.

The boy grinned. I gave her my shirt. I went three weeks with nothing on my back. Next summer I'll find her again.

Julia said, I wish you great luck.

She shut the door and took up the broom, and began sweeping with rough strokes. The boy's story had annoyed her; she imagined a crying native woman, wading into a frigid river, alone. She tried to turn her thoughts toward William: he would be home at sunset; she'd prepare soup with onions and the previous night's veal. Afterward she'd try to coax him from the sickroom. She could ask about the boy's stomach, or about ailing soldiers at the hospital. She could ask about hunger.

She stepped into the sickroom. The boy sat on the cot, grinning, his hands clasped over his abdomen. His auburn hair hung in knots at his shoulders. He offered Julia the empty teacup, but when she took it, he didn't release his grip.

It's not fair, is it?

Her breath caught; she attempted a smile. What isn't fair?

I've shown you my wound, he said. You haven't shown me yours.

What if I'd told William then? she wonders. If I'd told him then, he would have turned the boy out. If he'd turned the boy out, he wouldn't have begun his experiments. If he hadn't begun his experiments, he wouldn't have become so obsessed.

She closes her eyes, listening to raindrops patter against the carriage roof. Outside, a church bell tolls, seven hollow, lingering peals. Dr. Pearse clears his throat.

I could still be that eager girl, she thinks, with chamomile in my hair and a touch of rosewater on my neck.

She thinks, I should have told him then.

———

Winter's first storm arrived in October, a snow-thickened wind that gusted across the straits, rattling the cabin's doors and throwing sparks down the sooty chimney. Julia woke to find snow slouched against the cabin walls. Watery light filled the windows, illuminating a glitter of frost on the quilt. She crouched near the fire, her cheeks roasting even as her back prickled with cold.

She emptied the chamber set, turned the bed, swept the cabin, then gathered the smoky lamps. Finally she untied her apron and skipped in a figure-eight around the kitchen, until her heart was pounding. What shall we do this afternoon? she said, addressing the stuffed bluebird on the mantel. Shall we commission a hot air balloon? Perhaps fly to London—or Athens! The bluebird stared, head cocked. For the first time in her life Julia wished she were more religious; then she'd have a daily service to look toward.

A clatter rose from the sickroom; Julia paused, then began buffing the lamps.

She'd avoided the sickroom, during the past weeks. When the bell rang, she'd brought the boy's tea or lunch and set it on his table with a polite good-bye. His nightshirt lay crumpled on the floor; an empty teacup sat beside the bed; a vinegary tang hung in the air. The boy reclined on the cot, his lazy, toothless grin following her across the room. She shut the door on his plea—Ten minutes, *madame, s'il vous plaît*—and as she did, she felt a warm, infuriating flush.

Now she filled a basin with hot water and crumpled in a handful of chamomile leaves. She let the leaves steep, then bent over the basin and pushed her hair beneath the water's surface. Steam beaded on her cheeks as she counted to two hundred. She folded her wet hair into a towel, then took William's journal from his desk and opened it on the kitchen table, and poured a cup of tea.

October 17, 1822

8 o'clock, evening—*The boy dined on broiled mutton, bread, potatoes, and a pint of coffee.*

9 o'clock, 30 mins—*Worked open the perforation in his stomach and found a mixture resembling porridge, with an acid smell and slightly bitter taste. The boy complained violently of pain, but not hunger.*

11 o'clock—*All the chymified food had disappeared through the pyloric opening. The boy felt no traces of hunger.*

Satiety seems to occur early in the digestive process. However, hunger does not recur until after digestion is complete. This would seem to imply that the absence of food in the stomach is not the sole agent of hunger.

Fortunately, the boy's appetite is frequent, allowing regular experimentation. As Howell would say, He is a child of hunger.

Awake until dawn, unable to sleep.

> *Raging surf pounds against the shore,*
> *the ship tossed humbly, to and fro,*
> *and all observed from high above,*
> *by man, not God, whose knowledge grows.*

The door opened. William stamped his snow-caked boots, his cheeks glowing pink. Brutal cold! I think my hair is shivering.

Julia shut the journal and jerked upright. She pulled the towel from her head. Would you like a cup of tea?

He stood at the door, snowflakes glinting on his beard. He nodded at the closed journal. That isn't your monthly women's so-and-so, you know.

Julia was silent.

He removed his wet hat and coat, then stood at the table and paged through the journal to his previous night's entry. He read silently.

I apologize, William, dear, Julia said. I was curious, do you see? I should have asked you, I know, but I didn't want to appear so ignorant. I want to know about your experiments. Will you please tell me?

She watched his eyes fall to the poem; then a flush darkened his forehead. Why were you reading this?

I was curious, about the boy, and about your experiments. And your poems—I wanted to read your beautiful poems.

William's expression seemed to soften momentarily. He closed the journal and frowned at her. What happened to your hair?

I stained it, Julia said, for you.

Well, my dear. He cleared his throat. It's complex.

Yes. Please try to explain.

He stared at a damp tendril of hair resting on her shoulder, then followed it slowly to her face. There are many theories. Some believe the stomach acts like a mill, others believe it's like a stew pot. Others liken it to a fermenting vat—in the way it operates, the way it accomplishes digestion. No one knows for certain. There have been studies of dogs, and many hypotheses—but no one knows.

The boy is your experiment.

The boy is a *wonder*, William said, leaning over the table. Do you see, Julia? He allows me to observe, not simply hypothesize, the stomach's actions.

The bell clanged.

Stay.

William leaned back, smiling. Dear. He's ill.

Please, Julia said. He's not ill.

The bell rang again, followed by a soft curse.

I hear him walking in his room, when you're gone. And he rings for me during the day. When I arrive, he doesn't say a word—he gives me an insolent smile.

He's a boy, William said. Need I remind you?

He's not a boy.

William kissed Julia's forehead. Then he placed the journal in his desk drawer and disappeared into the sickroom.

She dashed her tea into the fire and clattered the empty cup against the table. Stupid boy, with his stupid grin and *voyageur* stink. Julia imagined him lying on the cot, feigning helplessness, while William bathed his wound and listened to his slurred complaints. When did William listen to her? When had he ever listened to her, besides that first night in Detroit, at the medical society ball, when she'd told him that doctors were fallen angels?

Muted laughter trickled from the sickroom. Julia leaned toward the sound.

The *mangeur de lard* are like animals, like rats. Truly! My first season, we paddled down the Ottawa, across the lake, then over grand portage to Rainy Lake, to the fort. You think it is cold here? There it was cold enough to freeze piss in midair.

William chuckled. Impossible.

The *mangeur de lard* turned back at the portage, so it was just the *hivernants*—seventy men, trapped in that fort all winter. I was sixteen years old—I woke every morning with my *boutte* in my fist. After dinner someone would take out a fiddle, and another would fetch a tin pan, and they would waltz. A few tied sashes around their necks, to dance as women. Men would argue with each other for the next dance, with the woman-men. Can you imagine how lonely, now? One morning I woke to find a woman-man in bed beside me.

Go on.

That's the end. It's how I lost these teeth, the fight. He lost worse.

A fatigued laugh, trailing into a sigh. Julia set a plate and fork on the table for herself. Let them laugh together, like schoolboys, she thought. Let them stay in the sickroom all night.

The boy's voice reminded her vaguely of a young man she'd once known: John Wells, a banker's son with a desperate smile. He'd sat across from her in church every Sunday, watching her with feral intensity. One morning she'd allowed him to walk her home; he'd taken her hand, his palm slick with sweat, but said nothing. On her porch, he kissed Julia's knuckles and whimpered, like a hungry dog, and pressed her fist against his chest; then he guided it lower, against his trouser buttons. Julia clenched her fist but didn't pull away.

Now a shout rose from the sickroom. I don't know, the boy shouted. *Non.* Are you deaf? I don't care.

William stepped into the kitchen. Is there meat tonight?

She nodded at the covered stew pot.

He hurried to the bedroom and returned with his pigskin bag. He opened the stew pot and took up a knife, then sawed off a strip of veal and laid it on a dinner plate. From his bag he withdrew a spool of thread and snipped a long string, then looped it around the veal. He knotted the string, so that it trailed from the veal like a kite's tail.

What are you doing?

An experiment. If I can convince the boy to let me.

You shouldn't hurt him.

He glanced at Julia with a confused, anxious expression. No, dear. Of course not.

He took up the plate and hurried to the sickroom.

Snowflakes whistled across the frozen windowpanes. Julia forked the veal and potatoes onto a serving dish, then sat watching fat trickle and whiten on the pewter plate. Finally she moved her chair beside the closed sickroom door.

Silence; a rustle of bedsheets; then the boy's whispered voice: Stop, *Docteur. S'il vous plaît.*

She woke that night to a groan of floorboards. She sat up: the bedroom was dark, save for a wedge of light flickering beneath the door. William's pillow was untouched. A cold prickle rose on Julia's arms; she stepped into slippers, then nudged open the door.

William spun through the candlelight, arms bent around an invisible partner. His eyes were closed, and a faint smile lay on his lips, as though he were lost in a pleasant reverie. His journal sat open on the table, a pen propped across the pages. Julia sucked in her breath as he whirled past, grazing a chair with his hip.

His arms snapped to his sides. What are you doing?

Julia smiled weakly. I had trouble sleeping. I heard a noise— the floor.

Go to bed, William said, taking up the pen and scowling at his journal. I'll bring something to help you sleep.

She opened the door wider. What's happened?

Nothing. Please: let me finish writing.

She stepped toward him, and his mouth tightened. She said, I want to read it.

Bruise-colored crescents lay beneath his eyes; a blot of ink stained his lower lip. His expression was drained but radiant, as though he'd just sailed alone across an open sea. Julia searched for her own reflection in William's stare. This once, she thought. Please.

You can read it, William said. And then you must let me finish writing.

Julia nodded.

He turned the journal toward her. She approached the table as if in a soundless dream.

October 13, 1822

The preceding four experiments seem to suggest that hunger can be allayed without food passing through the esophagus . . . and thus chymification

It would appear that nutrient

A simple Theory of Hunger: *that the sensation of hunger is produced by distention of the gastric vessels, and is abated by the replenishment of gastric juice.*

(This refutes Magendie's theory, and thus dozens of experiments will be required to prove the notion.)

Unable to sleep.

Unable to sleep . . .

What is man, That thou art mindful of him?

For Thou hast made him little lower than angels, and hast crowned him with glory and honor.

The carriage turns from the roadway onto a broad curving drive, the horses' hooves crunching into gravel. All of the medical society's windows are lit, with a soft yellow glow that lays shadows on the building's pilasters and shows smiling figures moving silently inside. Julia searches for her son's form as the carriage rolls to a halt behind a column of cabs.

"It should be a wonderful evening." Dr. Pearse rubs mist from the window with his jacket sleeve. "Drs. Heywood and Bostock will be here. And Dr. Genot—apparently he was in New Haven, delivering a lecture, and traveled here specifically for tonight's dinner."

The names cause a tickle of recognition in Julia: Dr. Heywood, of course, but Bostock and Genot? So many doctors, over the years, and often she hadn't cared enough to ask William their names. A ship's bell echoes, then a rank, fishy breeze drifts in from the river—and suddenly she remembers an apartment in Paris, with a tiered glass chandelier and pink marble floors. A dinner, to celebrate the European publication of William's book. Monsieur Genot, a skeletal man with a white pompadour, was leaning across the table. *Madame*, he'd said. Were you aware that something remarkable was occurring in your cabin?

A question to humor her, before the ladies were dismissed and the men spoke of weightier matters. Julia smiled politely.

Of course. I was worried—William's behavior was very odd.

Conversation trickled to a halt. William stared at her, his cheeks ruddy and loose, a wineglass suspended halfway to his lips. They'd long ago settled into a neutral coexistence, with William a shadowy visitor to Julia and her son's world. It was strangely agreeable: at least, she thought, they understood each other's needs.

She said, He thought only about the *voyageur,* Roleau. He became a different man.

Monsieur Genot murmured approvingly. William's gaze fell to Julia's dinner plate, then the balcony doors. He set down his wineglass and excused himself from the table. Julia listened to his heels click against the marble floor; then she felt a nudge against her ankle. Monsieur Genot was fixing her with a patient smile.

That night she lay awake in the dark hotel room, eyes closed, her tongue thick with the taste of wine. Flies droned and stuttered against the windowpane. William rolled onto his side and grasped Julia's wrist. I'm so sorry, dear, he said. For everything. Julia.

She murmured sleepily.

Dear, please. He shook her wrist. *Julia.*

She remembers the fragility of his voice. She bore him no grudge, she'd often told herself; why, then, hadn't she opened her eyes, let him kiss her fingertips, press his forehead against her chest? She remembers the hard flame of pleasure that burned inside her, as she listened to William's ragged breathing. She lay beside him, her own breathing deep and even.

"I was hoping you could introduce me." Dr. Pearse's hand is resting on the carriage door. "If you wouldn't mind."

"To whom?"

"Dr. Genot. I would be honored to make his acquaintance."

Julia thinks, You poor sad man. She says, "Of course," and steps down to the rain-slicked walkway. The front doors open onto the familiar arched foyer, the massive oak clock, a waist-coated Negro waiting to take her cloak. Ridiculous, she tells herself—nervous as a child, after so many years—but her stomach refuses to unclench.

"Did you know," Dr. Pearse says, "that the society arranged for the *voyageur* to come here tonight, from Montreal? He's still in fine health. Apparently he's unaware of the book's importance."

"Of course I know."

"I hear he refused to come, at first." Dr. Pearse frowns. "He requested nearly twice the travel allowance the society proposed."

A bubble of laughter melts Julia's tension. Good for him, she thinks, to benefit, finally, from being prodded and ogled— he should have demanded far more, long ago. William would have given him anything he asked.

She draws a deep breath and offers Dr. Pearse her elbow, then steps into the bright foyer.

In November a hush fell over the cabin; Julia found herself clattering dishes and slamming cupboards, to create an illusion of company. After lunch she bundled herself in scarves and walked down to the straits, the crusted snow scraping her calves, then stood watching dark figures trudge toward the garrison, slowly deducing if the person was William, or a soldier, or the boy.

He'd disappeared on the first Saturday of the month. Julia and William had dined at the major's house and returned to find the boy's room empty, his cap missing and a teacup shattered on the floor. On a drunk, she assumed, with his half-breed friends. She neatened his bed, then swept the cup's shards into the snow.

She woke the next morning to find William sitting at his desk, hands folded in his lap. The cabin's silence seemed to emanate from his open journal.

He's not back?

William grunted.

Julia glanced into the sickroom. She said, Do you suppose he's in town?

He was quiet for a long moment. Perhaps. Or he could have taken a sled to Pickford.

He's at Pickford, she thought, and felt a twinge of relief. She laid her hands on William's shoulders. He'll return soon, she said. Or you'll find another way to conduct your experiments.

You stupid barren girl. There's no other way.

She jerked her hands away.

How will I conduct my experiments? Find another *voyageur* and shoot him in the stomach?

Julia shook her head.

Or shall I experiment on myself?

No, dear, I can't—

William slapped the journal shut. He yanked his coat from its peg and stamped out into the frigid morning.

The days seemed to pass in darkness, the few hours of sunlight barely rousing Julia from her morning drowse. She let soiled laundry pile in the storeroom, and huddled beside the fire, watching maple logs hiss and snap. The fire blazed but seemed to emit no heat. She woke every morning to find ink frozen in William's inkwell.

On Friday she was writing to Susan when the rear door slammed. Her hands tensed; she wrote, *He is just now arrived back*. She eased open the sickroom door: the boy leaned against the wall, head lolled forward, a muddy yellow sash trailing between his legs.

His head rose; he grinned and stepped toward Julia, then stumbled to one knee. He groaned, then rolled onto his back. He yanked his shirt up to his chin.

The wound yawned, its crimson edges ragged and scabbed, a thick gray fluid sliding down his chest to a puddle on the floorboards. The boy pressed his hand over the wound, as if to force the fluid back into his body, then picked a lump of what looked like potato from the puddle and stuffed it into his mouth. He giggled, then took the bell from beside the cot and clanged it.

Let me help you, she said, please. Lie down.

He squirmed his shoulders onto the cot, as Julia shoved his legs over the side. His hair was matted with mud and tiny black pebbles. He smelled of liquor and pipe smoke and vomit.

She said, I'll bring you a cup of tea.

No, stay. *Julia.* He pronounced her name as three slurred syllables.

You shouldn't move. I'll get my husband.

He is trying to kill me.

Julia waited for the boy's laugh, but he seemed suddenly sober. She said, Nonsense. He saved your life.

He struggled onto an elbow. He does horrible things to me, Julia. He starves me. He puts things inside me.

His eyes were red-rimmed, and for a moment Julia thought

he might cry; then he broke into a giggle. *S'il vous plaît*, Julia. You're my *maman*. You're the one who saved me.

You're drunk, she said. It's disgraceful.

The boy grinned.

Why did you come back? If William hurts you?

His laughter stopped; he stared at Julia with an empty expression. He laid his cold hand on her thigh.

I'll bring you tea, she said.

S'il vous plaît, he whispered, Julia.

She moved her leg away. Her thigh tingled, as though it'd been pricked by needles.

The boy slumped on the cot. Don't bring me anything, he said. I'll be gone in ten minutes.

He was asleep when she brought the tea, and when William returned from the hospital, his eyes teary with cold. Julia waited until he'd removed his boots and was warming his feet at the fire, then said, The boy is back.

He stared at her; then his gaze flicked to the closed sickroom door. He's in there, now?

He's asleep. He was drunk when he returned.

William opened the door and peered inside, then quietly pulled it shut. He hissed, What did he say? Where was he?

I don't know. He fell asleep.

He stepped toward her, then spun in a pirouette, fists clenched. Oh, sweet Lord thank you, my God, thank you. He hugged Julia, pinning her arms to her sides, then kissed her cheek and nose and jaw, his beard a cold bristle against her skin. Sweet dear, thank heaven. He laughed noiselessly. Thank heaven, oh Lord, thank heaven.

William's entire body trembled, and as Julia hugged him a sob rose in her throat—for she had never made him tremble, never made him thank heaven or the sweet Lord, never made him dance with joy. His neck was suddenly damp with sweat.

She said, He touched me.

William's eyes were closed. When? What do you mean?

Here. She guided his hand to her thigh. He put his hand on me, like this.

William opened his eyes. He was trying to get your attention.

Julia shook her head. I moved away, I told him you would be here soon. Then he said he would leave in ten minutes. I said I would bring—

Wait. *Wait*. Why did he say he would leave?

Julia stared at him. I moved my leg away.

William's expression seemed to collapse. He paced twice around the table, muttering, then squatted in front of the fire. He began to laugh softly. Julia, he said, Julia, my dear Julia, my lovely dear. The boy is a *wonder*. He wiped his face, and Julia realized he was weeping. He said, We must keep him here, dear. He must stay a few more months. Do you understand? He *must*.

She said, What would you have me do?

He was silent for a moment; then he spoke her name softly, like a guilty prayer.

A coldness rose in Julia, her lips and fingers feeling as though they were carved from ice. She stared at the bluebird and lacquered tree on the mantel, their names refusing to appear in her mind. The window reflected her white form above her kneeling husband; outside, there was darkness and wind and forest and snow, for hundreds of miles. She wondered: *Why do birds fly south?* Because they need warmth. *Why do trees grow tall?* Because they love the sun.

Please, William whispered, Julia.

She smoothed his damp hair. The boy's presence radiated from the sickroom, like a distant fire. Beneath her coldness, Julia felt a flicker of heat.

She said, I'll speak with him tonight.

The ballroom is crowded when she steps inside, and loud with the murmur of conversation. She sees Dr. Heywood and his wife, Dr. Szegy, Dr. Monchaux; then she glimpses her son, Jacob, standing beside the string quartet, his orange hair slicked with rain. He sees Julia and grins as he raises a hand. Now he'll cross the room, his smile unbroken even as he searches her face for signs of worry. He'll offer her champagne, and when she refuses, he'll sip from his own glass, as if to prove it's delicious— as if she's a child, in need of encouragement. The thought causes a swell of happiness to rise in Julia.

She slowly scans the room. She doesn't know what the boy will look like; for so long she's imagined him as a pale, grinning *voyageur,* with knotted hair and thick, calloused fingers. But of course, he's no longer a boy, no more a boy than she's a young girl. What will I say, she wonders, when I see him? She wants to ask him if he still sings paddling songs, though he's surely too old to travel a river. She wants to ask him who he married, and why, and if he loves his wife, and if he's always loved her; and if his children are home, awaiting his return, or if they left long ago, to follow their own errant hearts. She wants to tell him that everything was due to him, all her bitterness and joy and sorrow and hope—but how to explain? She wants to ask him if his wound has healed.

I'll thank him, she thinks finally. Thank him for his warmth, during those cold months.

The crowd parts, and she sees a small, auburn-haired man slouched beside the window. A tremor starts in Julia as she moves toward him. Now she knows what she will say, as surely as if it's already a memory: she'll greet him, and bend to kiss his weathered cheek. She'll introduce him to Jacob, as if the two men were strangers.

"Monsieur Roleau," she will say, "I would like you to meet my son."

NOTE TO THE READER

All of the characters in these stories are fictional; however, some of the events have roots in historical fact. "The Indian Agent" was inspired by the journals of Henry Rowe Schoolcraft, a nineteenth-century ethnologist and Indian agent. Some incidents in the story were borrowed from his writings. The medical experiments in "Children of Hunger" were based on those performed by Dr. William Beaumont on Alexis St. Martin, in the 1820s and 30s, at Mackinac Island and elsewhere.

ABOUT THE AUTHOR

KARL IAGNEMMA'S short stories have won the *Paris Review* Discovery Prize and been selected for the *Best American Short Stories* and *Pushcart Prize* anthologies. His writing has appeared in *Tin House* and *Zoetrope*, among other publications. He is currently a research scientist in the mechanical engineering department at the Massachusetts Institute of Technology, specializing in robotics.